Worth

Also by **A. LaFaye**

A. LaFaye

Worth

SIMON & SCHUSTER BOOKS FOR YOUNG READERS
New York London Toronto Sydney

SIMON & SCHUSTER BOOKS FOR YOUNG READERS
An imprint of Simon & Schuster Children's Publishing Division
1230 Avenue of the Americas, New York, New York 10020

Book design by O'Lanso Gabbidon

The text for this book is set in Adobe Garamond.
Manufactured in the United States of America
10 9 8 7 6 5 4 3

Library of Congress Cataloging-in-Publication Data
LaFaye, A.
Worth / A. LaFaye.
p. cm.
Summary: After breaking his leg, eleven-year-old Nate feels useless because he cannot work on the family farm in nineteenth-century Nebraska, so when his father brings home an orphan boy to help with the chores, Nate feels even worse.
ISBN 0-689-85730-6
[1. Frontier and pioneer life—Nebraska—Fiction. 2. Fathers and sons—Fiction. 3. Orphans—Fiction. 4. Nebraska—History—19th century—Fiction.] I. Title.
PZ7.L1413 Wo 2004
[Fic]—dc21
2003008101

To Tom Magee, the first teacher to see
my worth as a writer. Thank you.

Acknowledgments

Thank you, David, for your continued support. I hope you called this one right. Marcia, I really appreciate your loyalty, insight, and direction. As always I am eternally thankful to God for the opportunity to be a writer and to share my stories with others.

Contents

Worth

1

Lightning in the Grass

Ma says you can hear the lightning in the tall grass before a storm. Haven't heard it myself, but she swears there's a crackling in the grass like tiny bolts of lightning traveling from blade to blade. I remember her warning me of it that day.

"Nathaniel James."

Hearing my name pulled me up short at the front door. "Yes, ma'am?"

Ma looked up at me with her tinker's eye perched in front of her forehead. "The lightning's sparking in the grass this morning. Better warn your father. I'll be out in a tick tock."

I nodded, stepping into the eye-squinting sunlight.

A tinker's work tunes up your senses. You spend so much time working with the tiny pieces of a clock that your eyes get to seeing the finest things. Ma could spot one of my brown hairs in a basket of rye bread. And with all that concentrating with your eyes, your ears get to concentrating too. That's how come my ma can hear lightning in the grass.

"Storm's coming!" I shouted to Pa over the fence as I came up to the barn.

Pa looked up from cleaning Vernon's back hoof. "Your mother hear it in the grass?"

"Yes, sir."

He dropped the foot, patted Vernon's flank, then stepped aside to stare up at the sky—as blue and clear as Ma's wedding sheets hung out to dry. "Either that woman's a diviner or she's got relatives in the fairy kingdom she isn't telling me about." Stretching his back with his fists pressed into his muscles, Pa said, "Well, guess this means we better get the hay in today."

"Today?" We had a field of hay drying in the prairie sun, but just one wagon, two horses, a few pitches, and our own hands.

"Anything left on the ground will get too wet to be of use, Nate. What we don't get in, we lose," Pa said as he led Vernon into the barn.

"What if it's only lightning on the way?" I asked, following Pa. Ma's ears never told her wrong about lightning, but sometimes it traveled alone, striking at the ground like it'd quarreled with its companions thunder and rain and built up a good bit of fire-spitting anger.

"Then we better get it in before it catches fire," Pa said, backing Vernon to the wagon. "And the sooner you quit flapping at the mouth, the sooner we can get out there."

"Yes, sir." I ran to lend a hand.

Within the hour, we were in the field, Ma and Pa pitching from the windrows on either side of the wagon, me packing it on the hay net, Vernon and Belle munching their share until Pa gave the hi-ya to move forward. He had those bays trained like a couple of hunting hounds. They'd chase their own tails if he told them to.

The sun baked me until even my skin felt stiff when I moved, but we still only had a quarter of the field brought in when the thunderheads rumbled in, casting long gray shadows and putting a nice chill into the air.

"Put some step into it, Nate!" Pa shouted. "We've got a storm chasing us."

And chase it did. The clouds swept in from the east. We picked hay to the north. The thunder kept threatening like a big old empty cloud clearing its throat. Made Belle and Vernon jittery. They went to side stepping and flicking their ears. The first lightning strike made Belle whinny. Ma yelled, "It's getting close!"

But we only had the wagon three quarters full on this run. The storm had us licked. Pa knew it.

Throwing his fork into the wagon, he yelled, "Better to save what we can, then risk it for what we can't. Let's bring this load in."

We pulled up to the barn as the wind picked up. Ma headed out to bring in the other animals and batten down the house. Pa jumped down, pitch in hand. "Get that net ready to haul, Nate!"

"Yes, sir!" My arms felt like they'd fly off with the next throw of hay, but I pitched it into the center of the net so Pa could haul it to the loft.

The storm heated up, the thunder booming louder, the lightning lashing harder, the air filling with the moist feeling that comes just before it rains. All that racket had Vernon and Belle fidgety. They kept jostling the wagon.

"Steady," Pa called out from the loft doors, but that didn't steady them none. He threw the hooks down into the wagon. "Hitch 'em!"

I scrambled to hook the net while Ma brought Dimple around to pull it. That old cow had eyes as big as a pitching ball at the fair. She stepped into the rope and began to pull, Ma leading her with a bucket of oats.

As the net went up, hay billowed out of one end. Blast it all. I hadn't got all the hay in the center like I should've.

"Get to cleaning, Nate!" Pa shouted through a gust of wind.

As I swept my pitch to throw the hay slop into the barn, lightning spooked the horses, and they jolted the wagon. I stumbled forward jamming my pitch in between the bed of the wagon and the side.

"What's holding you up, Nate?" Pa yelled, thunder backing him up.

"I got my pitch stuck."

Lightning filled the sky like a sudden flash of deadly sunlight. The horses jumped, jolting the wagon again. I turned around at the wagon's edge to give the pitch a yank.

"Well, get it unstuck," Pa said, pulling the hay net in.

Thunder crashed dead above me. The horses jumped forward. I fell back, breaking to the side, my leg sliding into the wheel. Then lightning struck ground, sending those horses toward the house and my leg into pieces.

My mind gobbled up the world in that instant, then spit it back at me in tiny little moving pictures—the look of the wheel turning all splintered and gray—the ground rolling by with rocks hopping up—my pitch tumbling to the ground and ricocheting. No sound. No feeling. Just a jumble of pictures all moving faster than rain itself.

The pain came with the rain. So white-hot and sudden, I thought the lightning had struck me. I suppose Ma and Pa came for me, but I don't recall. That pain yanked me clean out of the here and now to a place that stretched me out until I was thin enough to cover a prairie mile, each inch aching with a pain so sharp I would've died to make it stop.

Then a fog rolled in, misting me clean through—no pain, no thoughts, nothing but wet gray haze, like I'd been set adrift in a boat at dawn.

2

Clearing the Fog

The world tumbled in on me like hay from the loft door, each blade cutting with knife-sharp pain. Had no way to collect my wits. My thoughts spread out with the hay. Sounds rained down.

Crying.

Ma crying, the high, soul-deep sobs she cried when Missy died.

Shouting.

A man shouting. "Hold him steady!"

Pa saying, "There's so much blood," like he spoke from his sleep.

Couldn't keep my eyes frontwise. They kept spinning as wild as my stomach.

Man said, "I'm setting it."

Then lightning struck again, shooting up my leg and into my skull, sending me deep into the fog.

Woke with my mind filled with mud, my thoughts too dirty and slow to come clear. My stomach rolled like the turn of a wagon's wheel. My leg bones felt like metal heated up good and red. I panted to keep up with the pain. Didn't do me no good. Screaming didn't neither, but my mouth took its own leave.

"Gabe!" Ma called for Pa. Felt her arm around my head, her hands touching my chin and my chest. "You hold on, Nate. Hold on."

Hold on to what, Ma? I wondered as I slipped right out of the room to wherever it is a body goes when it falls asleep.

The pain woke me often, but most times sleep turned out to be heavier, pulling me right back down. When the pain won out, screaming carried me through, Ma holding me, cooing over me, calling for Pa.

Ma said it took over a week for that pain to give up its hold on me. Long about then, I woke up with a hunger so bad, thought my stomach might turn on the rest of my insides for a little something to eat.

Ma fed me soup, crying the whole time. Didn't have my mind on nothing but food and the ache in my leg that ran out of room with only a thigh, shin, and foot to fill, so it moved out through the rest of me. Took so much of me, I fainted before I could fill my belly.

But each day, the pain got weaker. And soon I could eat a meal without making Ma cry.

Had to lie pretty still, though. And not just 'cause moving felt like breaking my leg all over again. The doc said I had to lie stone still if I wanted that leg to heal as much as the body allows. He had it hanging in the air like a side a beef. Told me to lie still so the bones didn't move under my skin. What I really didn't like was how he said, "As much as the body allows."

"What you mean by that?"

He held his breath a second. Doc Kelly does that when he doesn't want to talk. Then he said, "Your leg won't ever mend properly, Nathaniel. There's been too much damage. Best we can hope for is that the bones grow back together strong enough to hold your weight."

"So I can walk again?"

He nodded slow. "But walking is about all you'll be able to do. And that'll be hard going."

"If the bones grow back."

"Right."

Half wished my mind would fog up again so there'd be no room for the new thoughts rolling in. I'd be a cripple. Couldn't run if a bear chased me. Might not even be able to stand. What's a man do if he can't stand? Sit around collecting dust while the rest of the world earned their living.

Ma took to telling me about hidden blessings, saying I should be thankful Doc Kelly had come to town to tend to his dying father. Not ten doctors in all of Nebraska would know to use traction. Didn't feel so blessed in that. He drilled a hole in my bone like a carpenter drills through wood. Had me trussed up in bed so I couldn't move. Said I'd be there for months. Where's the blessing in that?

But I kept my lips tight and my head nodding. She smiled, saying I'd be free to go to school once my bones mended. But what did I need with schooling? I had no designs on books and such. I wanted to be out there helping Pa.

He lost most of the hay. And the wheat and corn took a beating in the storm. Heard him tell Ma the Clemson cattle ran the fence again, ate up the north field of corn. We needed every ear of that corn if we wanted to make good on our homestead claim. Pa needed the money to pay off the bank for all our equipment and seed. And what was I doing? Lying around like a freeloader, watching Pa march out into the fields alone.

Ma helped when she could. When she wasn't nursing me like a little baby. I kept telling her, "I'm fine. Go help Pa."

She'd say, "Your pa could be in here helping me."

Truth was I hadn't seen much of Pa except through my bedroom window. He had no time for socializing. Went out before dawn. Came back at sundown. Ate, then slept.

And I tried to keep my mind on other things. Things that could give him a hand in some way. Ma did her part.

Nights she sat up to work on her tinkering, fixing clocks, pots, hand tools. Used to be, we delivered them after church on Sundays. Ma and Pa sat up in the front of the wagon while I ran the goods to the front door. Folks'd take the clock or whatnot, then nod out to Pa, saying, "Thanks, Gabe." They paid us in anything they could—cups, coins, eggs, fresh beef, even a dress one time.

Never told no one Ma did the tinkering. She learned it from her pa, but folks didn't take to women doing a man's work. Didn't seem right to me—if a thing's fixed, it's fixed. What's it matter who fixed it?

"Things work out fine for me," Ma'd say. "Keeps us in food over the winter."

Now tinkering is something a man could do even in bed. I asked Ma to show me how it's done. She brought me the old clock her grandfather built. "Take this apart. Find out how it works. Put it back together." And with that she walked out. No "This is how you do it." Just "Take this apart." At least she gave me some tools to use. Old ones she kept all tied up in a cloth pouch and tucked away in her tinker box.

Two years ago, we came to Nebraska with not much more than that old tinker box. Ma insisted on a wood house. Said she wouldn't leave home to live in the dirt. Pa had to sell everything we had to buy the wood and pay to ship it and us all the way to Nebraska on the train. So we started out with a nice empty wood house.

No windows. No doors. No furniture. We slept on piles of our own clothes.

Brought in most of our house by tinker trade. A fixed clock with a promise of lifetime repair brought us some dishes from an old woman who had a wedding set from her first marriage that her second husband didn't like. We got an old table for fixing a brush rake. The farmer put up quite a stink over having to bring the machine over to our place, but Pa said he could only work on it when he had the time away from farming. So Ma fixed it in the barn. Chairs came to us through piecework. Ma fixed pots and scythes and rakes and picks for eggs or some such, took what we needed, then traded the rest to Ralph Pitcher for store credit at the mercantile. We ate standing up for near to a year before we had all three chairs. Pa did his part too. He made our beds out of fence posts he got for helping Tin Harper put up a fence on his ranch. Haying on the McKinley place on Sundays earned us a few windows.

We lived by trade mostly. Come winter, Ma traded for food goods. By spring, she traded for shares of folks' seed. Tinkering kept us going, so I figured I'd do my share if I could get a handle on it.

But I swear a clock's got more pieces than a watermelon's got seeds. Took me a week of Sundays to get it apart. And I figured I'd have it back together long about the time I started growing chin hair. Ma didn't help me none. Pa didn't pay any attention.

Doc Kelly just shook his head and laughed as he checked for infection. "Skin's nice and pink."

"What am I, a pig?"

He pricked my toes. I howled like a penned hound dog. He asked, "Feel that?"

"Didn't the 'ow' tell you?"

"Told me your foot hurts, not if you can feel your toes."

"And what if I can't?"

"They may just fall off." He didn't so much as crack a smile.

My stomach filled with ice. "Pardon?"

"Your leg's got terrible circulation, Nate. Not a lot of blood's going to these toes." He rubbed them, making them burn. "Got to keep the blood moving or you could lose them."

Knew an old man back in Illinois who lost his toes to frostbite, walked like he had a stump for a foot. "Should I wiggle them?"

"No!" He looked like I'd threatened to skin him. "Don't you so much as twitch a muscle in that leg of yours."

"But it aches and itches and sometimes it hops on its own." When my muscles hopped, I near about tore a hole in my bed for the pain of it.

"Leave it be, Nate. It'll only heal if you leave it be."

And I left it be all winter long. Sitting up in bed, I listened to Pa fret as I tried to fix that fool clock. He figured we didn't have enough to seed the crops next year or pay interest on the loan from the bank to cover the money he wasn't able to pay back. Not to mention the help he needed, but couldn't afford to pay. Staring at all its gears, I daydreamed that if I could put it together just right, I might be able to wind it backward to the day when a stupid bolt of lightning took my whole life away.

3

What a Boy Is Worth

The sound of his boots told me Pa planned to go into town. Heard the crisp clomp-clomp of his Sunday boots. I counted back on my fingers—no Sunday hadn't come again. It was only Saturday. When he stepped into the kitchen, Ma spoke in how-dare-you whispers. I knew them well.

Back when Pa came home with his homestead papers, saying we'd be moving to Nebraska come spring, Ma'd let her anger out in short hot bursts only Pa could hear. We all slept in the same room back then, but Ma could whisper so slow and quick, I couldn't hear a word of it. But the pitch of it said she didn't take to the idea at all. And whatever had Pa going to town on a Saturday didn't please her any.

As Pa stepped outside, I heard Ma say, "He won't be sleeping in this house."

Who did she mean? The jingle of tack and the rumble of the wagon said Pa headed out for town so I wouldn't see him until noon to know just who Ma meant. Months in bed had made me half-crazy. The idea of not knowing itched in my brain until I was ready to scream.

"Pa taking on hired help?" I called out to her.

"No." The quick snip of her voice and the way she punched at the dough in the bowl I heard knocking against the table told me just how mad she really felt.

"Who's he bringing back then?"

"No one I've approved of."

"Would I approve of him?"

She fell silent for a bit, then I heard her snuffle in a breath—she'd been crying.

"Ma?"

I heard her step toward my room, but she didn't come in. I could see the shadow she cast across the doorway, her shoulders stooped, her head bowed. Made me feel thin. She whispered, "He's bringing home a boy."

I didn't understand. She'd already said he wasn't bringing home a farmhand. "What boy?"

"An orphan boy."

Could've been neck deep in snow for how cold I felt right then. I'd heard tell of those orphan trains that brought in city kids to be picked out of a herd on a church stage and brought home like a new steer. The Campbells got a new son that way after their boy was taken by the measles, but I wasn't dead.

"He adopted a son?"

Ma rushed into the room, her face shiny with tears. "No. Not a son. Just a boy to help around here."

Held my breath like it'd keep me from bursting.

"Nathaniel, your father and I have only one son. We'll always only have one." She tried to brush my hair, but I swatted her away.

"I'm not Pa's son anymore. He hasn't so much as said how do."

She folded her hands in her lap. "He has his eye on you, Nate. Comes in and watches you nights."

"He does?"

She nodded, pointing. "From the doorway."

"When it's dark and he can't see me."

Ma shook her head. "Nathaniel, Pa just needs another set of hands around the place. This is the only way he could afford it."

Funny. A steer you'd have to pay for, but a boy you could adopt for free. Not worth much.

Worth. That was his name. John Worth. He stood in front of my bed all bit up by mosquitoes and scratching through a new suit. Pa didn't buy him that, did he? The kid wouldn't even look at me. He just stared at the floor.

Pa turned him roughlike to face the bed. "This is our son, Nathaniel." Looking over my head, instead of at me, Pa said, "Nathaniel, this is John Worth."

We mumbled our hellos, then Pa turned him around to march him out of the room. "I'll show you the lay of the land around here."

Ma stood in the door, her arms folded over her chest, her eyes dead set on the boy, just pouring out the hate like she did every time she set eyes on Verna Crawford, the woman who said she'd watch over Missy while Ma and Pa worked down at the thread factory.

Missy choked on a piece of bread. Died while that woman was doing piece work for a shirtwaist factory. And all that woman could say was, "I've raised nine children and didn't none of them choke when I put them down with a little bread to chew."

Ma near about tore that woman's face off before Pa

dragged her out the door. The whole of it froze me to the spot, felt like a ghost standing there staring at that woman bleeding on the floor, the drawer she'd had Missy sleeping in dropped sideways behind her, empty except for the old pocket of Ma's apron Missy kept with her.

Mr. Crawford shooed me out the door and closed it behind me. Don't know how long I stood in that hallway before Pa came to collect me.

This time Pa had turned me into a ghost, sitting there staring at the spot on the floor where John Worth had stood.

But I wasn't going to let that no account city boy bury me alive. I'd show Pa just what I could do. Since Doc Kelly had finally cut me loose from that contraption, I could start moving around a bit, building up the strength in my leg.

The thing looked evil wrong. My left thigh had shriveled up to be as thin as my right shin. My left shin looked no bigger than the bones inside it. Had a big purple scar where the bone broke through the skin.

And the whole leg burned like wildfire when I so much as curled up a toe. And shake. That thing shook like a leaf in the wind. Not that the rest of me did much better. I'd been moving my arms, my right leg, and turning my body best as I could to keep up the muscles, but you can't do much with your left leg trussed up.

Had the strength of a butterfly. Near about passed out just swinging my legs over the edge of the bed. "Take her easy there, son." Doc Kelly ran to sit next to me. "You rush this and you're liable to just break the leg again."

"Heaven forbid," Ma gasped, covering her mouth.

"We won't let that happen, Mary Eve."

Wouldn't much happen if I didn't get stronger, but I couldn't do a bit that day except fall back into the bed and let sleep take me off. I dreamed of birds. Pigeons all clustered up on a ledge clucking away like only pigeons can, but the noise continued even after I opened my eyes in the darkness of night. Took me a bit to figure out I heard crying, someone crying on the other side of my bedroom wall. But the only thing back there was the lean-to where we kept the wood for the fireplace. Then

I remembered Ma's words, "He won't be sleeping in this house."

She had that boy sleeping in the lean-to like a dog. Well, as far as I was concerned, that's where he belonged.

4

Dunce Goes to School

Ma carried me to the table like a baby. I sat there with my leg tapping a tune on the floor of its own accord. Couldn't stop the thing, even with my hand squeezing the thigh. Pa filled up his plate double full.

"What are you doing?" Ma asked.

"The boy has to eat," Pa said, dipping the spoon into the mashed potatoes.

"When we're through. We're going to sit here and eat as a family."

Pa stared at her, his hand still on the spoon.

I watched John Worth through the kitchen window. He sat on the bench in front of the barn squinting into the sun like he was waiting outside the barbershop for a cut.

"Lead us in prayer, Gabriel."

Pa set his jaw, steepled his hands over his plate, then

said, "God, thank you for this good food. May you bring such bounty from our own earth in the months to come. Amen."

Ma finished the prayer in a whisper. I always wondered what she said, but didn't want to pry into what was between her and God. Especially since He and I weren't exactly on speaking terms these days. If He meant for me to be replaced why didn't He just kill me outright instead of busting me up and leaving me here to watch some strange boy take over my life?

We ate without talking. Pa kept his eyes on his food. Ma watched him, stealing glances at me, like her eyes would draw us out to look at each other, but if he couldn't even set eyes on me, why should I pay him any mind?

"Doc Kelly says Nathaniel should be fit for school in another month."

Pa hummed.

"No more reading after dark and figuring in fire ash. He'll have a real schooling."

"Fine." Pa chewed like his food might blow away if he didn't eat it fast enough.

"Are you in a contest, Gabe?"

"What?"

"You eat like you've got to finish a pie for a ribbon."

"Got work to do," he said, mopping up gravy with his bread. Standing with a wad of bread in his cheek, he slopped up another plate, grabbed a fork, then headed out.

Ma stared at the door. I watched Pa bring the plate to John Worth. That boy gobbled up the food like he hadn't had a meal in a month.

A month. That's how long it took me to be able to stand on my own feet without falling over like a two-legged stool. Walking made it feel like my bones had healed into blades jabbing into me, but any kind of pain was worth the chance to get out of that darn bed.

And Ma saw to it I went a lot farther than that. She drove me into town so I could attend school. Back in the city, I'd worked just like Ma and Pa to bring in enough so we could move back to our farm downstate. Locusts ate up all we had, left us with nothing to live on for the winter or pay the bank with, so Pa had to give them our farm and we had to move up to Chicago. Just until we had enough to buy back our land, Pa said. We came to Nebraska instead.

And now I had the chance to go to school for the first time. A soddie on the south end of town, the place looked like the earth had grown a wart or something. Didn't look like a building really. Ma talked to the schoolmaster, a Mr. Kennel, who nodded through everything Ma said without a word of his own.

"He can read and write and do his sums. I'm sure he'll fit right in."

The staring faces of the kids out front of the school told me different. They had the hard look of hate in their eyes.

"Need help in, Nathaniel?"

"No, ma'am." I slid out of the wagon, sure to keep my weight on my right leg. I prayed Mr. Kennel would ring the bell, so I could walk across the yard without everyone staring at me like they were watching a two-headed pig at the country fair.

But no, he finally decided he had a voice and started talking to Ma about the newest readers that told the teacher just what level a student is at, and how he'd be sure to help me settle in with the other boys.

The other boys closed in around me as I hobbled toward the door, saying, "How do, Wood? What brings you to town, Wood?"

They always called me Wood—in church, after

church, any time we crossed paths—on account of the fact that we Peales dragged that wood across the prairie to build our house.

Talking back usually led to shoving and shouting and I didn't know if I could pick myself back up, so I just kept my eyes on the door and made my way inside.

They left me a bench to myself, which suited me fine. What didn't suit me was the fact that little Penny Dale with her whistle-gap teeth could read better than me. Even the big boys in the back who only came to school a couple months out of the year could read better than I could. Mr. Kennel put me in the front with all the littlest kids. I looked like a giant hunkering down with elves. But those little folks knew things I didn't have a clue on. They'd held a pencil before and learned to shape their letters just so, but mine looked all wobbly and wrong.

I should've been studying up on these things while I was laid up in bed instead of messing around with that darn clock I hadn't even gotten half together yet. Well, truth to tell, I'd put it together a dozen times already, but not in any fashion that made it work.

I proved to be just as dumb when it came to school.

They'd all studied things like map knowing. Called it geo-something or other that made it sound like they were speaking in a foreign tongue. And plenty of them could. At recess, kids clustered up to eat their lunches, some of them chattering away in funny words I couldn't understand. Not that the English-talking kids took to it well.

They tore up the new Cordimas kids from Greece just on account of having peculiar names. The girl was Anemone. I guess that's a flower. Kids called her Pansy, Dandelion, Ragweed, any old flower name to make fun of her. Her brother Alexander yelled back at them in Greek. That just made the name callers shout all the harder. They called him Alexander the Grape.

They may have had a hard row of it, but even those kids from other countries knew more about the history of our nation than I did. Had no idea Benjamin Franklin had invented all that stuff—a stove, glasses of some kind, the first post office, and his own university. University was sure someplace I'd never go for how stupid I was.

By the time Ma came to pick me up, I felt like my brain was as shriveled up as my leg. I just wanted to go home and bury myself under the house, but no, Ma had me working on my homework before and after supper on account of Mr. Kennel telling her I had a lot to catch up on.

As I sat in bed, trying to make my letters look decent, I heard John Worth go into the lean-to chatting up a storm. Leaning in close, I heard him say, "Seen a rabbit today. Hopping right past me like I was nobody special."

Rapping on the wall, I said, "Who are you talking to?"

"Keep your ears to yourself!"

Ma stood up as quick as if I'd shouted in pain. "Is that boy yelling at you?"

Caught by surprise, I said, "No, ma'am."

What was I worried about? Wouldn't hurt me none if he got yelled at.

Ma slapped the wall. "Go to bed in there!"

He mumbled something, then fell silent.

Just be glad you aren't in my shoes, boy. He got to spend the day with Pa watching rabbits and I had to sit in a room of kids who hated me, looking like the dunce that I am.

5

Fences Inside and Out

Pa's voice woke me. "Can't even pull a teat. Can't tell a rake from a hoe. That boy has been living under a rock."

Huh. So I wasn't the only dunce. Pa showed me how to draw milk from a cow before I could button my own britches.

Heard Ma swivel in her chair, then say, "He's been living in the city among those street gangs that steal from anyone they can lay their fingers on. You saw what happen to Hester Feringeld. She had a week's pay plucked from her very pocket when she pitied a young girl in the street. That kind woman stopped to give the girl an apple and one of those dirty urchins came up and stole her pay. Her own children had what for to eat for a week."

"And just how do you think those children ended up on the streets, Mary Eve?"

"No-account families."

"Or tenement fires." Pa pulled on his workboots by the fireplace. I could see his back from my door. "John's family died in a fire."

Heard Ma swallow a gasp. "Was the boy hurt?"

"No." Pa stood.

"Then he should be counting his blessings."

"And I'm sure he is." Pa went out.

With Pa gone, I could see Ma staring into the fire with that lost look that came over her when she thought on Missy.

Me, I couldn't help myself. I started crying. Crying 'cause I knew just how John Worth felt about losing his pa. And the thought of losing Ma crushed me up inside.

"Nathaniel James!" Ma called.

"Yes, ma'am."

"Get your body moving. Breakfast will be on soon."

"Yes, ma'am."

My fingers shook as I got dressed, but it could have been my fear as much as fatigue that made them so. Looked up to find John Worth staring at me through the window, his dark eyes shining like rocks in the sun.

At that moment, I wanted to tell him how sorry I was that he didn't have a Ma and Pa, but then my own Pa called him from the barn. My mind spun like a weather vane in the wind. Just 'cause he lost his father didn't mean he had a right to mine. John walked off. I bid him good riddance before going to help Ma set the table.

Pa came in as I started folding the napkins.

"What you doing?"

I jumped. He hadn't spoken direct to me in months.

"Folding," I whispered.

He stepped forward, whipped a napkin away from me, then threw it on the floor. "That's woman's work. Don't you have schoolwork?"

"He can help me, Gabriel."

"He's not a girl, Mary Eve."

"And it won't make him into one to help around the house."

Pa pointed at me, looking me right in the eye. That look burned clear down to my belly. "You keep your mind on school."

"Yes, sir."

He marched out and didn't even come back for breakfast. Ma shook her head, putting a napkin over his plate and setting it in the oven. As Ma helped me up onto Belle, I could see John trying to pay attention while Pa showed him how to harness Vernon to the plow. But he kept looking to the house, probably wondering after his breakfast.

I stood there wishing he was riding Belle into town and I was standing shoulder up to Pa. I could harness Vernon before he had time to beat Dixie with that swishing tail of his. But no, I had to go make a fool of myself in school.

Ma pulled Belle up short before we reached the creek.

Resting her hand on my bent up thigh, Ma said, "Your father's as twisted up as this leg, Nathaniel. Hasn't been right in his thinking since you were hurt. Can't say what has him so back to front, but I'd guess he feels responsible."

"He didn't spook the horses."

"No, but he had you pitching that last bit of hay."

"Do you think it's his fault?"

Ma moved her hand to my shoulder. "No." Sighing,

she said, "But I sure wish there was a way to set his thoughts straight."

"Traction. We'll get Doc Kelly to put his head in traction."

Ma laughed, then set Belle to walking over the bridge.

Pa may have his thoughts in a knot, but Ma had pretty clear ideas in my way of thinking. She let me off by the mercantile so I could walk to school. No one would see me riding with my Ma holding the reins.

But sitting in school made me feel like she'd dropped me into a runaway wagon with no reins at all. Nothing they said made much sense. And I couldn't make my letters come out right to save my life. My Bs looked like Ps and I couldn't make my Os rounder than a dried up pea.

The place was like a root cellar—dirt walls, air choked up with must, and bugs. Bugs crawled all over the place. The floor, the benches. Little Milton Harper tore off their legs and stuck them on top of his straw hat. I found a creepy crawler in my notebook. Gave him a good finger kick into the window. Horace Danver seen me do it. Whipped up his notebook, picked himself a bug off the floor, then launched that little critter right into Katia Mavchek's hair.

She screamed, swatting at her hair like bees swarmed her. The rest of the kids laughed like they were watching a circus clown.

Mr. Kennel had Horace Danver standing up in the corner to think hard on his misdeeds, but he hadn't thought better of such behavior by recess. Started him a fight with Trevor Gantry right off.

"Get your cowpoke feet out of my shooting area!" He shoved Gantry away from his marbles. "Won't have you tromping all over my things like your cattle in my daddy's fields." Horace kept pushing, so Trevor pushed back, knocked him over.

Horace jumped right back up. Those boys charged into a heads-down-shoulders-locked tussle.

Folks circled them, shouting, "Get that land-grabbing cowpoke!"

"Cattle thief!"

"Fence cutter!"

Herder meets homesteader. Like asking a cougar to dance with a bear. They both fought for the same ground. Ranchers wanted grazing territory. Farmers needed room for crops. Even the call for water led to fighting. Does it go to the cows or the crops? Danver land backed up to the Gantry ranch, so those families drew their battle lines in the dirt—the Danvers screaming crop damage, the Gantrys shouting fence cutting.

We had the Clemson cattle to contend with, but Pa never thought of suing for damages like most folks. Seth Clemson helped Pa clear his land and gave us beef when we needed it. The range war didn't come to our place, but it sure tore up that schoolyard with those boys punching, kicking, and biting, the others cheering them.

You could say those boys danced over a grave. Last fall they found Calvin Danver face down and tangled up in a Gantry watering hole on the river. The Danvers cried murder, but the Gantrys blamed it on fence cutting and whiskey—found fence cutters and a bottle nearby. The Danvers shouted lie! But Doc Kelly said the boy didn't have no marks from a struggle and he had plenty of whiskey in his belly. The idea of cutting into a dead body made me shiver, but I was glad the whole thing hadn't led to a lynching like it had over in Clay County when those Taylor folks got strung from a bridge after they burned a homesteader in his barn.

Of course, what Doc Kelly said didn't make the Danvers hate the Gantrys any less, and that hatred had those boys drawing blood until Mr. Kennel came and yanked them boys apart.

Had them leveling the dirt floor with boards when we went back to lessons, something I would've had to do with my leg trailing me like a tail. I watched Trevor, seeing him with his head hanging low, moving all slow and angry, but still looking like a regular old boy. Hurt me to watch him like that and there wasn't a thing wrong with him. Made me feel dirty shameful, knowing how Pa saw me hobbling around the place. I figured Pa hated seeing me torn up. Made him feel worse than I did watching poor Trevor leveling the floor like some drifter slaving for a night's rest in a bed. Must have made Pa feel so bad he couldn't even look at me.

Ma said he blamed himself. But why should he? He didn't send that storm. He could never know that lightning would spook the horses. I was the one dumb enough to get the pitch stuck.

Felt my chest filling with knots.

Darn it all. What good's it do to go dwelling on the past? God's not going to change what's already been done. Like Ma said, "He should count his blessings."

Ma sure was a blessing to me. And she wanted me to do well in school, so I tried to forget about Trevor and do my best to remember all I knew about ciphering, but those little tykes who sat in front of me ran circles around me—adding, subtracting, multiplying, even dividing. Went home as tired and stupid as the day before.

And so the spring passed—me making a fool of myself in class, the herders butting heads with the homesteaders, Ma tinkering up a storm. The only hint of happiness I got was when I heard Pa shouting at John Worth for doing something city dumb again. Each night, that boy came into the lean-to just a-talking away like he had himself an invisible friend, chatting on about all he'd seen that day in hawks and prairie dogs and such.

I didn't bother saying nothing about it. He'd just

deny it again. Instead, I blocked him out and tried to make my way through the McGuffey Reader Mr. Kennel had assigned me, so I could move ahead of the little tykes before I turned twelve and truly became twice as old as any of them.

6

Done with the World

On Sundays we all went into church, me riding on the seat between Ma and Pa, John riding in back where he belonged. The boys taunted me, saying, "How's your brother there, Wood? He clean your boots for you too?"

But I didn't pay them any mind. I just took my seat between Ma and Pa and smiled at that empty spot between Pa and John Worth. He might live at our place and work with my pa, but like Ma said, he was a farmhand, not a son. Not my brother. Just a boy who did my work. Thinking such made me feel small. It didn't do me no good to remind myself he wasn't part of the family.

The way he stared up at Pastor Emerson, looking like he'd cry if he heard the word "father" one more time, all hunched shoulders and gripped hands, made me shrink up inside. I couldn't hate him—he felt as heart small as I did. But my Ma and Pa sat right next to me. I could reach over and touch them if I didn't think Pa would cringe.

The whole of it made me dizzy. Leaning back to clear my mind, I remembered just where I was. Just how I got there. Why'd God have to break me up inside? Why'd He kill John Worth's parents? If He'd just left well enough alone, we'd each have our pa back. We'd be happy. Part of a family, not sitting there all alone in a mess of a people.

Folks around me, they prayed for rain and good crops and good health. I prayed God would hurt ten times as much as He hurt me. Let Him get busted up inside so He feels He's worth no more than the bugs I crushed under my boots at school. See how He finds the life He's given me. Spit on Him. That's what I wanted to do.

But Ma, she prayed as tearful and thankful as ever. Thanking Him for keeping me alive and giving her husband good help and good health, and tinker work, and a strong growing garden. The list just kept on going until I wanted to remind her of how she buttoned

Missy's body into her finest green wool dress, saying, "It's like dressing a doll."

Was she thankful God let her little baby girl die? What was the hidden blessing in that, Ma? Did you count your blessings that day?

I didn't see her lips so much as move at Missy's funeral. We'd taken her down home to be buried with Granny Washington—the bank couldn't take the family plot away. And we stood there on the corner of our old farm under the oak trees, wishing we never had to come home. Is that why Pa took us to Nebraska instead? So he'd never have to look down on little Missy's grave again? I know I could go a lifetime without setting eyes on that little lamb Pa carved out of wood.

And the more I thought about it as Pa drove us back home from church and I sat in my room piled under all my schoolwork, the more I never wanted to do anything.

I never wanted to see Pa take a step to the side so he'd miss me as we passed in the yard. Never wanted to grit my teeth against the pain of leaning down to do something as simple stupid as tying my own darn shoe. Never wanted to feel the stares of folks who heard my leg tapping its cotton-picking tune. Never wanted to recite my 7s like a baby in front of all those kids who could figure any old numbers they cared to.

And I never, ever wanted to read another darn book like a stuttering old fool. So I threw that stupid reader out the window and buried myself in bed. God could have His stupid old world. I wanted nothing more to do with it. Amen.

7

The Evil in Dark Truth

On account of my mood, Ma thought my leg had me down in the body, so she brought me my supper in bed. She sat beside the bed trying to feed me, but I took the spoon, saying, "I'm fine, Ma. Just sore. Go on in and eat."

What did lying matter to me? I just wanted to be as alone as I felt. Sitting there, eating my stew, I heard John muttering away in the lean-to, but he wasn't prattling on. No, this time he spoke real slow like he might be praying. I put my ear to the wall to hear just what he felt he had to pray about. And I heard, "J-a-ck s-at un-d-er the t-ree."

That boy was reading my book. If you could call the sounds he made reading—more like a baby oogglie googling really. Finally, someone who read worse than me. Felt like teasing him, but he knew I'd thrown that book out the window, probably heard me stuttering my way through it. Once again, my thoughts on hating him turned tail and ran straight for me. How was I ever going to get anywhere in school throwing my books out the window?

The old clock stared at me from the dresser like a worm-eaten stump, all useless and dead. Tinkering came about as natural as school for me. I just wanted that piece of junk out of my sight. When Ma came for my dishes, I said, "Take that clock with you. I can't make the fool thing work."

Ma put her hand on the clock. "Your Uncle Jaspar lost half the pieces before he gave up."

"Uncle Jaspar tried his hand at tinkering?" I couldn't believe that the man who could top a tree faster than most men take to shave ever thought on something as slow and small as tinkering.

"Nearly put his hand through it." Ma laughed. "Made him so mad he smashed a pocket watch to scraps."

Seeing the road Ma took, I rolled my eyes and threw my head back to wait for her to saunter up to the idea that I might not be good with tinkering, but I just hadn't found my calling yet. "Well, I can't be a lumberjack, Ma. I got this dead tree of my own." I slapped my leg.

Facing the dresser she'd bartered for, Ma stared at me out of the corner of her eye. The straightness in her back made the stiffness settle in my chest for a second. I even wished I could chew those words right out of the air.

But I didn't get a talking to. She just took that clock under one arm, the dishes in the other hand, and walked out, leaving me in cold silence to give my guilt plenty of room to grow.

What would she have said anyhow? A man with a bad leg needed book learning to find his place. To be a doctor or a lawyer or a newspaper man, you needed to go to university. I'd be Pa's age before I ever saw the end of grammar school. What chance did I have at college?

The answer rang back in my head like Ma had slipped in there with me unawares, saying, *No chance at all if you don't bury all those sour thoughts and put your mind to good use.*

Yes, ma'am, I thought, digging out my tablet to try my hand at figuring.

Rain kept everyone close to the house that Monday. Ma had pots to mend, so she kept to the brick oven out behind the barn, heating up metal scraps to melting so she could build little dams out of that steaming hot liquid. I'd seen her do it with her thick gloves and her stiff smock all made of leather, her skin almost as red as the flames.

But she didn't want me getting all wet and risking a fever, so I stayed out of school and in the house. Pa spun into a fixing frenzy repairing tack, mending his boots, and moving from room to room tending to all the things he'd let go during planting season. Most days when weather kept Pa inside, he'd talk his way through his plans for things around the farm, telling me how many men he'd bring in to help with the harvest, how he'd pay them back in kind, stretching his plans out between us to see how they sounded. But that day, he kept to himself, sometimes stopping to stare in at the wall in my bedroom. Or maybe he was staring at John, who probably sat in the lean-to reading my primer like I should've been doing.

Instead, I tried to keep up in all my other subjects and help Ma shine up her tinker tools. Erasing and cursing my way through my sums, I made Pa look up from his repair work on the kitchen floor. "What has you rubbing that paper back to pulp, Nate?"

Felt kind of prickly in the skin to have Pa talk to me. "Dividing."

His eyes took on the look of glass, reflecting back to something I couldn't see. After a short while, he pointed at me with the file he'd been using, "You keep yourself sharp in that school. A man with a head for numbers can run a real farm, figure his returns with more than guesswork, plan things out so he's expanding, not living from harvest to harvest."

I didn't see what knowing numbers had to do with farming, so I said, "You can do all that, Pa."

He laughed, tapping his temple, saying, "I don't have any more up here than old Vernon."

A smile crept across my lips, not 'cause I thought it was true, but because the idea was so silly. Pa frowned and I bit my lip.

Standing, he moved to the door, his eyes on his accounts box. "You learn what you can from that Mr. Kennel, Nathaniel. The world can't make a workhorse out of a thinking man."

We both knew Ma kept our accounts. Pa'd never learned much of numbers or letters. Grandpa Peale couldn't spare the boys on the farm for any schoolwork. When Ma offered to teach him to read, Pa'd say, "Hard work shrinks your mind. Got no more room up here for book learning."

"Ma's good with numbers, Pa. She could teach you."

Pa turned, his face hard. "I know what your mother's good at, and I don't need reminding." Sliding the file in his pocket, he headed for the door. "Better check for flooding."

So much for talking with Pa. I'd made him so mad he'd rather slop around in the mud and the rain than talk to me.

Like two fellows on opposite shifts at a factory, Pa went out and Ma came in. From the downy feathers on her apron, I figured, she'd been tending the new chicks. Those little critters can go stir-crazy in a long rain and peck each other to death.

Ringing her hair into the dry sink, she asked, "Where's your pa going?"

"Checking for flooding."

A loud bang in the lean-to turned her attention. Stepping to my room, she knocked on the wall. Felt my chest go tight over the idea she might yell at him, but she said, "Come on in and warm yourself!"

He called back, "I'm all right."

"I said come in and I meant it!"

"Yes, ma'am."

The door opened and he came in looking like he'd been hay jumping—leaping from the hay loft into a mound of hay—all mussed up hair, hay bits, and twisted up clothes.

Ma asked, "What have you been doing?"

"Nothing." He stared at the floor, his lips twitching, his eyes all misty. He'd been crying. Had a bad dream maybe. Thrashing about on a hay bed can leave you in such a state. Ma had to pluck many a hay bit from me when the fever twisted me about back in my bedridden days.

"Nothing looks like a dangerous occupation with you." Ma walked around him, then pulled a chair up to the hearth. "Warm yourself."

"Yes, ma'am." He sat down, his back as straight as the chair.

The whole room felt as stiff as he looked, until a rap at the door shook things up. Ma opened the door to let in the rain and a soaking wet Seth Clemson. "Good day, Mary Eve. Gabe around?"

"Checking the fields," Ma said, latching the door. "Steam yourself dry there, Seth."

He chuckled as he went to the fire. Tipping his head to me and John, he said, "Trouble brewing along the river, Mary Eve."

"What sort of trouble?" Ma asked, pouring him a cup of coffee.

"The Danvers found over a dozen sheep dead and bound up in fence wire."

"That's a shame. Sheep would run into a river and drown to outrun a wolf, but I can't see that many sheep twisting themselves up in wire no matter what's chasing them."

"True enough." He took a sip, nodding. "The pasture's nothing but mud, so you can't tell a footprint from a mud puddle, but they found fabric from a shirt caught in the wire. They're saying it was the Gantrys that killed them."

Ma put a hand to her chest. "How can they tell? One plaid's as good as another. What makes it a Gantry shirt?"

"Ten years of fence fighting." Mr. Clemson put the cup down.

John stared at me, his eyes wide with confusion. Fence fighting didn't mean a thing to a boy from a city, but I knew Mr. Clemson spoke of cattle trampling crops, then turning up lame or missing, a Danver boy drowning on Gantry land, and now the killing of Danver sheep.

"They talking of lynching?" Ma asked.

Mr. Clemson nodded, saying, "*Then* their talk turns ugly."

I didn't realize I'd held my breath until John startled it out me, saying, "I seen a boy hang once. Stole a steak from Hankee's Butcher Shop."

We all stared at him like he said he'd seen a ghost.

Suspicion flared in Ma's eyes. She asked, "You saw a child hung for stealing?"

John nodded, staring off for a second. "His whole body shook like he was trying to get free. They said he was too small to break his own neck." He laughed, a twisted up laugh that made me shiver inside and out.

No one moved. The weight of his story froze us all in our place.

"That's sinful wrong." Mr. Clemson shook his head.

Ma hugged her arms. "The poor child."

"Not so poor anymore," John said. "You don't need a full belly when you're dead."

The truth in dark things seems as evil as the things themselves just for being true. And I wondered just how dark John Worth had to be inside to say such things.

Pa came in to stir things up again. Funny how one person entering a room full of dark things can send them flying.

"Seth! What's got you out in this soaker? Got a field of corn drowning out there. Don't need to be fishing any friends out of puddles."

"Danvers think the Gantrys are killing their sheep."

"Is the sheriff on hand to smooth things over?"

Seth said, "You know the Danvers don't trust Baker after he backed Doc Kelly over Calvin's death."

"Then who has a hand in cooling things down?"

"Not enough folks by my reckoning. I thought we could go over there and talk some sense."

"Gabriel?" Ma looked at Pa like Mr. Clemson had spoken of going off to war.

"Calm yourself, Mary Eve." Pa patted her arm. "Won't come to nothing if we can quiet folks down."

"Doesn't matter who puts the noose around their neck. If you're in a lynching party, you're guilty of murder."

"Won't come to a lynching, Mary Eve." Pa motioned to Mr. Clemson to head out.

"That won't be in your control, Gabriel. You can't promise that."

Letting Mr. Clemson leave first, Pa turned to smile and nod. "I'll do my best."

Pa seemed happy to be going. I didn't see the pleasure in it—going off to step into a war between two families. But other folks saw glory in such things. I'd seen boys acting out the shootout at the OK Corral like those Earps were killing the devil himself.

What's the glory in shooting a man dead, even one as lying evil as Ike Clanton? Dead men can't make up for what they've done wrong. And there's never any guarantee you won't end up dead yourself. Look at Morgan Earp. Died in a saloon like a common gambler caught with too many aces in his hand.

The possibility of Pa getting hurt had us all as nervous as cooped up chicks, rushing around, trying to keep busy, snapping at anybody who made a sound. Ma set to making a meal for us, forever moving, probably trying to outrun her thoughts. John made a show of sweeping cobwebs from the ceiling. I crated up Ma's tinker tools, trying to keep my mind afloat, never giving a settling chance to things like lynchings, drownings, and sheep killings. And as I watched him strike at the walls with that broom like he chased after bats, I could only imagine what John Worth tried to outrun that night.

8

The Weight of Guilt

Ma sent us to bed after supper, but I couldn't sleep. The wait for Pa made my muscles ache. The rain had finally stopped, but the wind carried on, whipping the prairie grass. Singing cut through the wind like laughter through a prayer. It didn't fit. Seemed wrong somehow.

Pa and Mr. Clemson sang as they tromped across the north field. The pitch and roll of their voices broken up by laughter said they'd been drinking. I heard Mr. Clemson shout, "I better head home before I forget the way." He laughed.

"Don't go getting caught up in any fence now!" Pa yelled back. Mr. Clemson laughed again.

Pa whistled his way into the house. "All's well," he sang to Ma. I heard him trying to yank off his boots, but his hands kept slipping, sending his elbows into the wall. He laughed, then tried again.

"Did whiskey save the day?" Ma asked, her voice dark and low.

Pa growled.

Felt it in my chest. I pulled away from the light coming in my door, my eyes fixed on Ma as she stepped to the fireplace.

"What would your rather have—men who've come to blows? Or men who've had a few drinks?"

Ma crossed her arms over her chest. "Heaven forbid you should consider talking."

"Talking?" Pa laughed. "You mean like you and I are now? I'd rather have a drink!" I heard him drop into a seat, then stand right quick to say, "I might even settle for a punch in the eye."

Shuffling across the room, Pa said, "Go on, Mary Eve." Through the doorway, I could see him facing Ma, poking at his eye. "Take a swing!"

Just the thought of it had me pressed against the wall, praying Pa would stop talking.

"I'm not about to strike you, Gabriel."

"Oh, but you'd like to, wouldn't you?" He stepped

closer, his face all twisted by drink and anger. "Hit me for leaving our girl with that woman. Slug me for dragging you out here! Punch me for pushing to get that damn hay in!"

Ma turned away. "I don't blame you, Gabriel. You do enough of that on your own."

Pa's voice fell quiet as he waved at her back. "I can see that."

"I can't look at you like this."

"Like what?" Pa moved out of sight. "Drunk and stupid? Only half of that changes when I sober up." I heard something metal struck to the floor in clattering pieces. Pa shouted, "Won't find me fixing things! No, I break them. Kill them even."

Ma turned to face him. "You did not kill her!"

"Oh, then who lost that farm? Who borrowed money he couldn't pay back? Who dragged us to Chicago?"

Ma's voice thinned, as if she'd suddenly become too tired to speak. "That woman killed our child. And God will reckon with her for it. Don't you take on the weight of things that aren't your doing. You didn't call down those locusts. And you certainly can't control a storm. These things happen. We can't change them."

"No, we just march back out into the fields and plant again like there will never be another storm, another swarm of hungry pests, another twister. So you'll forgive me if I need a little something every now and again to forget just how stupid I am to believe I just might get ahead this time."

He stormed into the bedroom, leaving Ma at the table.

In the silence, my stare seemed to take on its own weight as if it could pull Ma into looking at me. Telling me Pa was wrong. He could get ahead. The crops would come in. We would pay off the loan and have enough for the next year's planting. And in five year's time, we'd own our land free and clear, never need the bank again. But my stare had no such weight. Ma simply got up to pick up the pieces of the clock she'd been fixing for Earl Baker.

9

Inviting In and Letting Go

Everyone pretended the kitchen battle of the night before hadn't happened, but a stiffness hung in the air, making it hard for things to move around, even words. As I stepped out of the bedroom, Pa loaded up his plate and John's from the fireplace, then turned to go out to the barn. Ma didn't say a word. When I tried to speak, my words didn't hold up. They just sort of drizzled out. "Are the Danvers . . . Are they . . ."

Pa walked by me without blinking an eye.

"Gabe."

"We've got a lot of work to do. No time for a sit down." Pa balanced John's plate on his arm to open the door.

"Gabe!" Ma called again, but Pa walked out.

She looked at me to say she'd heard me and Pa

should've answered, then brought my plate to the table. "Eat up."

Sitting down to face the window, I watched Pa bring the plate to John, who smiled. The boy spoke, then laughed. When Pa sat down beside him, he was laughing too. What was so funny?

"Nate." Ma tapped the table, saying, "Eat up."

An idea dropped from my mouth before I had time to think on it. "If John ate with us, Pa wouldn't be in such a rush in the morning."

Ma cast her eyes on nothing in particular and blew on her coffee. "Is that so?"

She gave that question a little time to settle into my mind. Having John at the table meant having John at the table. He didn't belong there. We didn't even have a chair for him. But it'd bring Pa back to the table. More important, I could hear what they had to say to each other, know what John Worth said that made Pa listen. Made him talk. And even laugh.

"Don't get much chance to see Pa these days what with school and all." I hadn't even stepped into the barn since the storm.

Ma looked at me, her lips thinned. "And having the boy here?"

I glanced out at John. "Won't harm nothing, will it?"

Cutting into her egg with a fork, Ma said, "We'll see."

And see we did. At supper that evening, Pa brought in the milking stool for John to sit on. I imagined him looking like a knee-hugging child with his chin just coming over the top of the table as he sat on that little stool, but Ma set one of her delivery crates on top.

John Worth said "please" and "thank you" and ate with his mouth closed. Pa said hardly a word through the whole meal. It felt like sitting in church when the bishop came round to remind us we were miserable sinners. And I sinned all right, just praying perfect little John Worth would turn on the crate wrong and go tumbling to the floor. Even thought of chewing with my mouth open and letting all the mashed up food fall back onto my plate.

Stiff in her chair, Ma ate little, said nothing, and didn't look up when she passed food. My brain dribble of an idea almost felt worse than having to hear Ma and

Pa yell at each other. I prayed Pa would think better of it, take the milk stool back to the barn after supper and never bring it back. But he didn't. He got up from the table, wiped his face, then left, saying, "I better check the rest of the fences before dark."

John scrambled off his stool, knocking the crate down. "I'll bring the animals in." John rushed out before Pa could respond, but I saw him shake his head like he had when I picked up a seed bag from the wrong end and dumped it on the barn floor.

That gave me a smile, but Ma slammed things around like she'd rather break the dishes than clean them. I helped, but she didn't so much as look at me.

Part of me wanted to know why she hated John Worth so much. I knew why I hated him, but did Ma see him the same way? Was it just because he reminded her of the kids who robbed Mrs. Feringeld? Or that Pa didn't get her approval first? In her mood, I didn't have the courage to ask. And she didn't need to tell me to go study. As soon as the table was clear and the dishes were clean, I headed straight to my room and closed the door. I wanted to be free of all the anger in the air. I even opened my bedroom window to let it all float out over the fields.

10

A Flower with Slices for Petals

After Mr. Kennel made a new rule that fighting at recess meant plugging chinks in the soddie or fixing the roof after school let out, the boys split up at recess—the Gantry crew shooting marbles in one corner of the schoolyard and the Danver crew shooting in another. But both lots seemed to be doing more talking than shooting, almost like they were planning something.

All I wanted to do was keep out of their way. And after a time, I knew just how to do that. Each day, Mr. Kennel read a poem before he rang the bell. When he called recess, he followed us out the door with his desk chair, set it by the door, then ate his lunch. When his meal was over, he'd pull a book from his vest, a collection of Keats poems. I'd seen it when he leaned over to correct my sums or, should I say, to show me just how many I'd done wrong. Well, each day he'd read one of those poems then reach down for the bell he kept at his feet, calling in a stampeding herd of kids with me hobbling along behind like an old heifer who'd gotten snared up in some barbed wire on her way in. The kids all snickered when I dragged myself into school after everyone had come in and found their places.

To give myself a little peace, I waited for Mr. Kennel to pick up his book, then I headed for the school door, knowing I could get inside before he called in the herd. Even gave me enough time to reach my seat.

One day, I found a kind of flower on my bench in that dank room. Someone had left an orange on a hanky in my spot—peeled and opened like a flower. Oranges are Christmas fruit, not day-to-day, giving fruit. Whoever left me that juicy present meant something real special by it, but I didn't know what. Couldn't find no note nor any sign the giver wanted me to know who it was. I folded up the hanky and set it in my pail before anyone could see what I had. Didn't want anyone begging for my orange or teasing me for getting it.

All afternoon I sat wondering who could've given me that orange, my mind settling on folks in turn. Theo

Harper dropped worms on my head from the hill over the river when I went fishing. The Campbell boy didn't like me on account of the fact I didn't treat John regular—orphan defending orphan, I guess. The Kerensky twins used to shove me back and forth on the boardwalk in front of the mercantile if they caught me there alone. Margaret Planck said I smelled like cow dung. Pretty much all the kids hated me and those who weren't spending their time hating me chose up sides between the Danvers and the Gantrys and hated each other. And when they weren't fighting in the schoolyard, they were gathered in clusters, hatching their next attack.

The little kids didn't pay me much mind but to laugh at me for being dumber than a sheep. So I couldn't figure who'd give me a kind word let alone something as true special as an orange. Looking over the room again, I realized I'd skipped right over those new kids from Greece. Maybe one of them gave me the orange for not calling them any names?

"Mr. Peale." Mr. Kennel smacked his ruler down on my tablet. "Perhaps you'd do better in your studies if you paid more attention to them."

"Yes, sir," I said, putting my eyes on my tablet, but

his slap had sent my leg to jumping. The whole room filled with laughter. Sneaking a peek at the Cordimas kids, I saw that they didn't laugh.

"Back to work," Mr. Kennel shouted, and the room fell quiet.

When school let out, I waited for the other kids to run home so I could walk to the mercantile to meet up with Ma. Setting out, I kept my eyes on my feet.

"You need repair?" Anemone made me look up. She stood on the edge of the path over the creek, pointing at my shoes. "My father, he is . . ." She bit her lip to remember the word in English.

"A cobbler? He fixes shoes?" I pointed at my shoes like an idiot.

"Yes." She nodded. The smile told me she'd given me the orange.

I dug in my pail to pull it out. Offering it, I said, "Want to share?"

Her smile grew. "Yes."

We walked to the mercantile together eating the orange.

"When our ship went to New York, Mana bought the oranges. We have too many."

People didn't buy too much fruit. I figured she said that so I didn't think she was sweet on me or something.

"It's good." I hadn't tasted an orange since the Christmas we moved to the farm in Goshen. I was six.

"Hmm." She hummed, sucking a slice.

"They have a lot of fruit in Greece?"

She laughed, holding her hands up. "All the fruit you can eat!"

"What else?"

"Water." She spun. "Everywhere. And trees. Such beautiful trees. All is green but the mountains with their faces of stone."

"That sounds so nice." I'd never seen a mountain except in pictures. Why would anyone want to leave such a place?

"It's the best place on earth." She smiled, then laughed. "But Nebraska is very nice."

I smiled, mostly because Nebraska was no match for an island at sea, but also because she said Nebraska with a Nee at the beginning and it sounded funny. "It's better than living in a desert, I guess."

"Nate." Ma startled me, appearing in front of us like a ghost. I hadn't been paying any mind to where we

were going, but looking up I saw that we'd made it to
the mercantile. "Who's this?"

"Oh, Anemone Cordimas, meet my ma, Mary Eve
Peale."

"Mrs. Peale." Anemone nodded her head.

"Anemone, the nymph who refused to yield to the
wind."

"Yes." Anemone smiled to have someone say
something about her name that had nothing to do with
a flower.

"Good to meet you, Anemone, but we best get home
for supper."

"Yes. Good to meet you, Mrs. Peale."

Anemone's accent made all the words sound like
new. She made the end of our name sound like a
musical note. I liked that.

"Thanks for the orange," I whispered, in case anybody from school might be listening in.

"*Parakalo.*"

"Come again?"

"Uh-uh, you're welcome. In Greek."

"Oh." I nodded. "Thanks!"

We waved and went our separate ways. As we rode

home, I asked Ma what she meant by what she said about Anemone's name. She told me that there was this Greek story about a little spirit called a nymph that tried to outrun the wind and was turned into a flower. Said the Greeks had hundreds of that kind of story to explain how things came about. I decided I'd have to ask Anemone about those stories in school.

But for the night, I just wanted to enjoy the feeling that somebody liked me. That warm-in-the-heart feeling I hadn't known since we left the farm and I had to say good-bye to Benny Saddler who lived down the road. I lay in bed thinking it was probably the first time I'd been happy for a good long while. Then John Worth had to go and ruin it all by having a rip-roaring nightmare.

I knocked on the wall to stop all the racket.

He bolted up, making the bed bump into the wall, saying, "Who's there?"

The fear in his voice caught me tight between hating him for ruining such a good feeling and wanting to say something nice so he wasn't so scared. It kept me silent.

Heard him breathing heavy for a bit, then he

started mumbling to himself as he settled back into bed.

I just felt empty all over again. Wishing I'd be able to talk to Anemone again the next day, I fell asleep with the sweetness of oranges in my mouth.

11

Cutting Fences, Building Ties

Fence cutters struck under the cover of night, snipping through barbed wire and spurring the cattle to stampede into the fields. The bellowing shook me from my sleep. Rising, I could see the dusty cloud of horns and backs trampling through our corn.

Pa ran out the front door, screaming to scare them back. Ma's cattle calls echoed his as they ran for the barn. Pounding on the wall, I rousted John. "Hurry, bring a coat!"

"What's happening?" John asked, his face ashen as he met me in the kitchen.

Grabbing his coat, I yelled, "Someone's let the cattle through. We've got to herd them back!"

As Pa and Ma tore out of the barn bareback, Pa called, "John, get Seth Clemson over here!"

"I don't know where he lives!" John shouted back, but Pa headed into the field, hollering and waving a coiled rope to scare the cattle east.

Mr. Clemson lived on the bluff over the river nearly a mile away. I never would've made it there before dawn. I grabbed John by the shoulders, surprised to find I stood taller than him, shouted the directions, then shoved him on his way. He ran, his white nightshirt disappearing into the darkness.

As Ma and Pa drove the cattle onto the slope toward the river, I stood in the door yard, waving madly with my coat and John's to shoo stragglers toward the road. We'd never get them back through the narrow opening in the fence line, but we could get them off our property.

Before Ma and Pa could clear the cattle out, Seth Clemson thundered in with a small posse of cattle hands to round up the rest, dropping John at my side before charging into the field. John stumbled and shook as if he'd been dead center in that cornfield when the herd charged through the fence. Knowing they had more capable hands at the ready, I dragged John into the house.

The boy couldn't even walk straight, so I dumped him into a chair. His legs trembled more than mine usually did. A quick tinge of revenge sunk under the weight of my pity. What had scared this kid enough to make his bones quake? A kid who'd seen a boy hang.

"What happened?"

"Happened?" He stared at me like I'd asked why he feared the devil. "The river valley filled with cattle as I headed for the bridge. Thought they'd run me down."

Cursing myself for not sending him further south to cross, I set to warming him a little water to calm him down. Ma always fixed me up a little water with a stick of cinnamon when fear had me jumping like a bug.

John didn't speak, he just panted down his fear while the makeshift tea brewed, then took the cup with a nod as I said, "It'll quiet you."

Gripping the cup, John said, "Never been in the country in the dark like that. Thought the ground might swallow me up."

John's words pulled me to the street outside our apartment on the night Ma sent me after medicine for Missy. She'd been wailing sick for days. Ma walked the floor with her all hours, so Pa worked double shifts to keep their wages regular. No one but me could go for the medicine, but the idea of traveling the streets at night had me gasping for breath by the time I'd reached the stoop. Thieves and killers lurked in the shadows of the street. I'd seen the crowds circling the dead in the mornings, heard the wailing in the halls when a second shifter lost a pocketbook to quick hands in the dark.

I couldn't move fast enough between the pools of light under the street lamps. Even the distant clomp of a horse's hooves sent me running like a hounded rabbit. Knowing John's fear made me feel closed in somehow, but I couldn't just let him sit there and shiver.

Taking a deep breath, I said, "Felt the same way in the city at night."

"Not me." John shook his head. "Isn't an alley I can't map out. A street I don't know like the teeth in my head."

My own head filled with memories of footpaths, burrows, bushes, and faint rises I'd grown to know on the prairie, faint reminders of our old home. "You'll learn to know the land here just as well."

John huffed in disbelief, then spoke as if reciting, "Can't take the city out of the boy to put the country in."

"Who told you that?"

"Your pa, every time I try my hand at something."

I flashed to Pa saying, "Where'd you go after you cleaned the stalls, Nathaniel? Looks like a rat's heaven in there." He never showed me how to clean a stall, he just handed me the pitch, saying, "Clean this out," then walked off. Made me feel dumber than a pig with half a brain.

An idea rose up in my throat. I nearly choked on it, but I let it out in a whisper, "I could show you a few things."

"Yeah?" John scoffed. "I hope you're better at farmwork than you are reading. Or your pa might as well ship me back to New York now."

"I wish he would!" I shot my hand out and dumped the cinnamon tea into his lap, hoping his legs hurt as much as mine did as I marched outside.

My anger carried me out to the field. Pa stood beside Vernon, staring at the mess. The corn looked as if it'd been chewed up by one of those combines we'd seen at the state fair. Only our corn hadn't grown to pickable yet. And it never would.

I heard Pa whisper, "Curse him to hell."

I knew Pa spoke of the man who'd cut through that

fence. I felt pretty much the same way, not only about that man who had cut into what little we'd had to live through the winter and pay back the bank, but also about John Worth, who'd pretty much trampled my life down like so much corn.

12

War and Myths

In the early dawn light, I tried to train my mind on the walk with Anemone to block out the yelling from the kitchen, but I couldn't.

"You have to do it, Gabe," Ma said with a pleading in her voice.

"I am not suing my own friend!" Pa yelled back. "He has his own bank notes to pay."

"It's your legal right. His cattle ruined your crop. He owes you the money for it."

"I sue for that money and who do I call on when I need help?"

"He'll understand, Gabe."

"No, he won't. He may think he does, but when the money wears thin, he'll be thinking on what he had to hand over to me and how much grazing land I'm taking

up with crops, and we'll find ourselves in a feud." Pa
paced as he spoke. "That's what this is about. The
Gantrys want every farmer at war with the ranchers.
Then again, it could be the Danvers for all we know.
Both families want blood. And they'll shed the blood of
bystanders to get it. We're heading for war, Mary Eve.
War."

The scent of war even filled our schoolhouse soddie,
with boys shoving and shouting in the yard, the girls
egging them on with taunts. And it wasn't just a
choosing up of sides for the Gantry-Danvers feud.
Dales went after Plancks, Kerenskys locked horns with
Harpers—only the townsfolk stayed out of the fight.
Apparently, the phantom fence cutters had struck all
around the territory, stirring up trouble between every
farmer and the neighboring ranchers. Pa had read the
wind well. A war was rising off the horizon.

And I hid from it like a yellow-bellied coward,
keeping my mind on figures when it wasn't wandering
back to the musical note Anemone Cordimas put at the
end of my name. At lunch time, I found myself
standing by the old log where Anemone and Alexander

ate. Didn't say nothing, just stood there like I expected to be invited over.

Kids made fun of their lunch as they passed, but I kept my mouth shut.

Looking at me, Alexander growled, "We have no oranges."

Anemone swatted him, then yelled at him in Greek.

"I wasn't looking for an orange." But I had a mind to make his eye swell up like one with a good swift punch. "I—I thought maybe you might have a book on them Greek stories about nymphs and such."

"Myths. They're Greek myths." Anemone smiled.

"Yeah. A book on Greek myths."

"Why do you want them?" Alexander asked. "To make fun of them?"

"No, to read them. Ma says you've got a hero called Hercules who killed a big old monster that had a hundred heads that grew back when he cut them off." Ma'd told me about that fellow on the way to school that morning. I'd asked after the myths to get her mind off the crops.

"The Hydra," Anemone said. "Hercules killed the Hydra."

"Yeah, I'd like to read about him."

Alexander leered at me, but he didn't say nothing. He didn't trust me, but his sister sure did. She said, "Walk me home from school. I will ask my father if I can loan you the book we bought in English. That's how I learned to read in English. We have the book in Greek and English."

"Oh, well." I felt stone stupid. Here this little girl could read in two languages and I could barely read in one. "I don't want to take away something you're studying."

"You are not. I study American books now." She tapped her reader.

Alexander huffed.

"Okay, then. I'll walk home with you."

"With us." Alexander stood up.

"Of course." I pointed over my shoulder. "Kennel's about done with lunch. I better head in before the herd stampedes."

Anemone looked at me in confusion, but I didn't have the time to explain. First because her brother looked about ready to crush my head. And second because the foul mood in the air meant I could really get trampled if I didn't get inside before the bell rang.

Horace Danver and his crew had taken to gathering behind the soddie, talking in low growling whispers that seemed to work them up into a stampeding frenzy. They'd charge out of the soddie like they were ready to tear it apart. I had to keep clear of them, so I sidled inside.

I swore I'd read that myth book cover to cover to make up for throwing my reader out of the window. And I'm known for keeping my word. That promise kept me moving even with Alexander staring holes into my head on the way to their house. Even when Anemone and her brother went inside, leaving me standing out front like a delivery boy waiting for a tip.

Anemone near about ran outside with it, her face red as clay as she handed it over. "Mana says to remind you to always treat something borrowed as you would the person who owns it."

"Sounds decent." I nodded, taking the book. "I'll do that."

A woman appeared in the doorway, a pan in hand. "Your *mpampas* is fixer. Yes?" She shook the pot by the side; the handle rattled in the base of it.

Took me a second to catch her meaning. She was asking about my pa being a fixer. Or maybe it was my ma? "Yes, ma'am."

Opening the door, she said, "Needs handle fixed. Can he do this?"

Taking the pot, I said, "Yes, ma'am."

Smiling, she said, "Good."

Anemone grew even redder. "This is Nate. Nate Peale, Mana."

Wiping her hand on her apron, she offered it to me. "Good to meet you, Mr. Peale."

"Good to meet you, Mrs. Cordimas." I shook her hand. "But I best be going. My ma's waiting for me at the mercantile."

"Go, go!" Mrs. Cordimas shooed me off.

Holding up the book as I hobbled off, I said, "Thanks for the book, Anemone!"

"Parakalo."

I headed to the mercantile with the book tucked under one arm, the pan under the other, bone happy to be thinking about nothing more than reading up on a fellow who cut the heads off an evil snake.

13

Words Through the Walls

Pa didn't come to dinner that night, said he'd be supping with Mr. Clemson to iron things out. Ma didn't say much until John slipped getting onto the crate and sent it and the stool clattering to the floor. Turning on him, she yelled, "Pick them up and sit in the chair!"

"But . . . ," John stuttered, the stool in hand. "It's . . ."

"But nothing. Do as you're told!"

John set the stool to rights and grabbed the crate to put it on top, then slipped into the chair. If he didn't look so scared, I might have been powerful mad for seeing him sitting in Pa's chair. Add Ma's anger and I just wanted to eat and be done with the meal so I could head to my room and read.

That book had fancy pictures like the ones that came

with the calendars I seen hanging up in the druggist in Chicago. Mrs. Kempki sold those pictures for a nickel. Our neighbor, Mrs. Feringeld, bought one and framed it in the pieces from an old thread box, then hung it over her table. I loved looking at that lady doing her wash at the river, she seemed so darn happy to be elbow deep in clear water. But that book did those calendars one hundred times better. It had one of those fancy pictures on each page. And they showed the wildest things. A man with a horse's body where his legs should be, tiny little ladies that had wings big enough to carry them in the air, and a guy with a bull's head. That fellow was called Minotaur—a monster kept in a crazy maze by some fellow named, well, I couldn't say that fellow's name if it was tattooed to my tongue. I just called him Dead because his name started with Daed, which is close enough to dead. See, not only did that book have fancy swallow-you-up pretty pictures, but it had big, easy-to-read words, except the names, so I could actually read the stories. Took me forever, but they would pull you along good. Still, I had to read them aloud to keep track of what I was reading. And I read like that for night after night. But my favorite story was still the one about Dead and Icky. I reread it every night.

That Dead fellow, he not only built the maze that kept the bull fellow from getting out and killing people, but he built wings for himself and his son, Icky-something, so they could escape the king who kept them captive. And they flew up high into the sky. Icky got so curious about the sun that he flew too close. Those wings just melted and he fell to his death.

"He did what?" John asked though the wall.

"Huh?"

"Read that part again about Icky getting too close to the sun."

"You've been listening?"

"It's a real good story."

"Good enough for you to get your own book."

"And how am I going to do that?" His voice got louder as he leaned closer to the wall. "You're the one who gets to go to school. I only get to read books that get thrown out the window."

"That's my book and I want it back."

"Are you two fighting in there?" Ma shouted from the other room.

"No, ma'am," we yelled together, afraid she'd tan us if she had to come in and break it up. Or at least that was what I had in mind.

John whispered through the wall, "I'll give it back if you read me another of those stories."

I stared at the book, knowing it wasn't a fair trade. He didn't have no right to keep my book. But he'd said something that settled like a cold rock in my heart. "You're the one the who gets to go to school." His words echoed in my head, tumbling into all the things he'd said to me.

John shivering in a kitchen chair, saying, "Thought the ground might swallow me up."

He was afraid of the country and all the dangers he couldn't understand, just like me in the city.

Then he said, "Can't take the city out of the boy to put the country in."

Pa thought he was stupid. Just like Mr. Kennel couldn't believe I had any sense in my head.

And that awful night he talked about the boy hanging, saying, "His whole body shook like he was trying to get free. They said he was too small to break his own neck."

All these things made John's life as dark and lonely as mine.

"Did you know the boy who was hung?"

"What?"

"The boy you saw hang. Did you know him?"

John fell silent, then he said, "Tossed nickels with him, but no, I didn't know him."

Didn't know why a boy'd toss a nickel, but I figured I'd asked enough already, so I picked up the book, then reread the ending of the story of Dead and his son Icky. From there, we read about Hercules killing that snake with his friend Eye-o-laus. It's spelled Iolaus. Starts with an I and ends kind of like Santa Claus, so I figure it's Eye-o-laus.

I read until my eyes started to blur, with John chirping in with a question here or there.

"I've got to go to sleep."

"All right." John sighed. "Can we read again tomorrow?"

"We'll see." I closed the book and blew out the lantern, but I lay there wondering if maybe the quiet feeling inside me just might be the start of something good.

14

Running and Blood

I'd been reading up a storm, and since Pa went to meet with Mr. Clemson, a storm was brewing between Ma and Pa, but they didn't say a word about it, even in whispers. Then one morning, Ma had an I-won't-even-look-at-you way about her as she cooked breakfast. She didn't even sit down to the meal, just went straight from serving to washing dishes. I kept my mouth shut for fear of saying something that'd start a feud right there at the table.

"Going in to talk to Mr. Carter at the bank." Pa seemed to be talking more to his plate than to us. "Help around the house today, John."

"I don't need any help," Ma said, without turning from the sink.

Pa took a swallow-the-anger sigh, then said, "Then

you can go back to cleaning up the cornstalks like we did yesterday."

"Yes, sir."

Pa got up from the table and walked out without so much as changing into his Sunday clothes.

John started shoveling in his food as soon as the door closed behind Pa. His plate clean in a flash, he stood, saying, "Thank you for the meal, ma'am." He ran for the door.

Afraid of her answer, but knowing I should, I asked, "Need any help with the dishes, Ma?"

"I said, I don't need help." Her words bit into me, making a day inside an ugly idea all around.

"Yes, ma'am." Looking through the window, I watched John go to the barn.

Going outside didn't mean I had to cross paths with John and his citified ways. I could clean the stalls or feed the animals, maybe even slide onto old Belle and have me a look around the place. "I'll just step outside then. See what's what for a change."

"You do that." Ma kept her eyes on those dishes.

I headed out.

Took a coon's age to cross the dooryard. Stepping

into the barn felt odd, like all that dust settled inside me somehow, making me feel dirty. Dirty for not being out there every day helping Pa.

Didn't feel right being there now. Like I was invading the place or something—a gambler in a church. Couldn't get the bridle on Belle fast enough. Using the stall door, I climbed up on her back, then rode out. My leg took to aching right off, but I pushed the pain down and headed for the riverbed. Those cattle had trampled everything in their path, saplings, grass, and crops alike. I could see Gavin Tussler riding the fence line over at the Clemson place—knew him from his bright blue scarf, even from that distance. Probably making sure no one got any cutting ideas on the Clemson place. Him and the other fellow I could see riding east, but they'd need an army of fence spotters to patrol even one ranch.

From the bluff, I could see our place, a field of corn torn up, the hay rising up, fields of corn growing green in the sun. Looked like a marred-up painting to me. And for all I'd know of it, it might as well be a painting. Come harvest I'd be sitting up in the house like some dried up old man while everyone worked themselves to a happy ache by getting the job done.

Done. That's what we Peales were. Done. Done in. Done for. Even with a good harvest on the remaining corn and the hay, we'd never bring in enough to pay off the bank. No matter what Pa might be saying to Mr. Carter that morning, he had to be echoing a passel of other farmers. No way could that little country bank carry us another year.

We'd be packing up another house. Leaving it empty in the wind like our farm down in Goshen. Where would Pa take us next? Would he bring John Worth along? He'd be an extra set of hands if we went to factory work again. The thought of standing at a machine all day made my leg throb to the point of hopping, which spooked poor Belle.

I cooed to hold her steady, but she shifted, making my leg swing against her and hop all the worse, sending the idea I wanted her to get going and howdy. She shot off, nearly knocking me to the ground, but I righted myself as she flew down into the riverbed.

For a bit I hated her. Hated her for taking off. Hated her for spooking and dragging me into that wagon wheel, for bouncing me around like a sack of rocks. But then a rush of air woke me up inside, showed me the freedom of watching the world go by at a run.

Before long, I laughed into the wind, loving the quickness of it. I might not ever run on my own two feet, but I could put four under me, then ride to beat the devil in a foot race.

I let Belle run herself out. We ended up at the Gantry watering hole, sweating and thirsty. I didn't dare get down for fear I couldn't get back on, but I let Belle drink her fill. The shine on the water made it look alive. But I couldn't help but imagine old Calvin's face down among the rocks on the outer edge.

Why'd folks have to be such damn fools over land?

Didn't seem right for anyone to die over lousy old dirt. That stirred-up ugly feeling of not being able to do nothing came back, dogging me all the way home. But what could I do to change things? Not much unless old Zeus himself came down and granted me the strength of Hercules and a set of old Dead's wings to fly up in the air and watch out for any of those fence cutters. I could swoop down and knock some sense into them with a big old club, maybe even send them sailing on home to land in a hay mound or something.

I laughed at the thought of it. Me flying through the

night like some crazy old bug, knocking those fence cutters into the air like they'd been thrown from a horse. The idea of it still had me laughing as I headed through the torn up corn.

Suddenly, it started raining stalks. Flinging them away, I shouted, "What the—?"

"Laugh at me, boy, and I'll knock you off that horse. Cripple or no cripple!" John shook a pitch at me.

Reining Belle up short, I yelled, "Don't threaten me, Worth. I'll run you down like a rabbit." Turning Belle, I stood ready to trample that boy.

"You just try it!" He pointed the pitch at me.

With a hi-ya, I sent Belle charging, wishing I had it in me to run that boy down, but she ran past him, giving me the chance to jump him from above. Knocking the pitch away, I tackled him into the stalks. Punching hard to keep him on the ground, I felt the rage of it pushing through me like a fever, but this sickness gave me strength, pumping my fists with a fuel that burned hotter than coal.

John didn't have much to fight back with at first. I'd knocked him over, my body blocking one arm, his body falling on the other. He twisted to pull them free, trying his darnedest to block the blows and land a few of his own. He landed a head-ringing blow to my eye, but I had him bloody and screaming by then.

It was the blood that stopped me. The shiny red of it. Somehow made me think of the surface of the watering hole. The peace of it. The death. I pulled back, dragging myself away.

John sat up spitting. "Happy? Happy now? You can beat me like an alley dog! Little old cripple boy can whoop me at everything!"

I had my hand over a rock in a flash, but the tears in his eyes kept that hand still.

"Don't you call me 'cripple'."

"What should I be calling you, then? Don't go thinking you're any Hercules, jumping me like that. How could I defend myself?"

I laughed. "That's just what I was imagining. That's what had me laughing. Thinking on being Hercules, flying down to stop the fence cutters."

John blinked against the blood in his eye. "You weren't laughing at me?"

"Didn't even see you until you yelled."

He flushed red. "Oh."

Dirty, bruised, and bleeding, we two fools started laughing. Each of us hating the other for being what we couldn't be. Lot of good that did either of us.

15

Death and Doorways

As if someone had yelled truce, John stood up, then offered a hand. "Need help up?"

"Well," I looked at Belle grazing nearby, "unless I expect Belle to drag me home by the reins, I guess that's my only choice."

He shook his hand.

I grabbed it. He yanked me up, but I nearly pulled him down. Probably looked like a strange kind of wrestling match, the two of us pulling on each other in the field. John finally got me to my feet.

He stepped back, shaking his head.

"What?"

"You are one rough tough." He laughed. "You'd kick some tail in king of the hill."

"Excuse me?"

"Round my neighborhood, if a kid wanted to prove himself a tough, he'd declare himself king of the hill. Didn't even need a hill really, he'd just stand there and take on anybody who thought they could knock him down." He wiped the corner of his mouth with his sleeve. "Tried it once. Had my clock cleaned."

"So, you're no tough, huh?" I turned to head to the house.

"Nawh. That was my brother, Tommy. He could take down a bull with his bare hands. That's what my pa used to say."

A brother. John had a brother. "Was it just you and your brother then?"

He shook his head, his eyes getting all distant. "Had three sisters too. All slept in the same bed. I can still see them, their faces all lined up over the edge of the covers, shouting, "Morning, Johnny Cakes!" He laughed, then stopped to say, "That's what they called me, Johnny Cakes."

Chilled me to think on all those folks dying in a fire—the beast that ate you whole.

John walked ahead as I whispered. "I had a sister." Wasn't sure he heard me, but I just kept talking, "Wasn't much over a year old when she died."

"How'd she die?" he asked, real quietlike.

"Choked."

"My ma had a sister who fell through the ice and drowned when they were young."

I shivered, but we talked death all the way to the house. People in our families who met their ends by fire, choking, drowning, and the blade of an axe, like my Uncle Paul who cut his leg clearing land and bled to death right in the spot where he meant to build the curing shed. A funny way to introduce a person, but odd as it may sound, I felt like I knew a piece of John Worth when we stepped through the doorway into the house.

16

The Tears That Bind

Ma near about sent our hearts through our mouths with the yell she let out when we walked in. "How dare you!" She swooped in, grabbed John by the elbow, and dragged him toward the back door. "How dare you take a hand to my son!"

"Ma!" I shouted as John protested with, "But, ma'am. But, ma'am."

The whole of it made me jumpy inside and out as I tried to move fast enough to get between Ma and the back door.

But she beat me there, throwing the door open, then tossing John into the room like he was some mangy raccoon that'd broken into our house. "You can pack your things. You'll be gone by morning."

Slamming the door, Ma kept moving, bustling

around the room, moving this and that, ranting to herself. Unable to hear me as I pleaded for her to listen. "'He'll be violent,' I said. I've seen those boys on the street hitting and biting and kicking like animals. I won't have it in my house. I won't have it!"

Finally I just took in all the air I could, then let it out in one big holler: "I hit him!"

My outburst spun Ma around. Seeing me standing there, my hands in fists, she said, "Come again?"

"I hit him. Jumped off the horse, knocked him to the ground, then beat him until he bled."

"Nathaniel James Peale!" The full name called meant I had a tanning coming, but I didn't so much as flinch. I had it coming and anything would be better than being thrown out like an animal. Ma leaned over me, shaking me by the shoulders. "How could you?"

I stammered, but no words came out.

"Raising your hand to another human being makes you no better than a hooligan." Ma started to work herself into a sermon, then stopped real sudden. The look she gave the back door told me the wrong she'd done John had just set in. Covering her mouth with an open hand, she said, "Oh my."

Now was not the time to speak, so I kept my peace as she stepped real slow over to the door. Opening it to show nothing but darkness, she stared in, whispering, "John?"

His voice drifted out all low and angry. "I'm not street trash."

"Come here."

He stepped into the light, his face wet with tears. "I come from a good family, ma'am. A church going family."

"John." Ma put her hands on his shoulders. He started to cry again. "John."

"Yes, ma'am?"

"I'm sorry to have accused you of something you didn't do." Turning toward me, she said, "And Nathaniel . . ."

I stepped up. "Sorry I whooped you."

"Nathaniel."

"I'm sorry I hit you."

Ma led him to the table. "Now let me take look at you and get you cleaned up."

John slumped into a chair. "My mother, she didn't allow no fighting either. Not even with my brother and me."

Ma went to the sink for water and a towel.

And I started to really see what I'd done to John. Cracked his lip so it swelled up like an earthworm struck with a shovel—all purple and oozy. His left eye looked as bruised and swollen. He had cuts on both checks and his chin. He looked so bad I had to turn away.

Ma saw me turn and said, "You should be the one to help him, Nate." She handed me the water bowl. "Take a good look at your handiwork."

He winced and even yowled once, but John let me clean him up because he had his mind on better things. His ma. "Yeah, if I fought with my brother, she'd tie our shoes together and make us go around like that for a day. And if we so much as shoved each other, we'd get another day." He laughed. "One time we spent a whole week like that. Got so bad, I ended up following him around even after she untied us."

That story made us all laugh.

Then John caught Ma's eye, their smiles faded, and he said, "I miss her till it chokes me." Just like that he went from laughing to crying so hard he couldn't breathe. The suddenness of it sent Ma forward, like she was catching somebody who'd taken a fall. She even held him, but that wasn't enough. He slid out of the chair and hugged her so hard her neck turned red. The pain of it twisted me up inside until I cried.

Ma carried him in to his room and stayed there whispering to him for the longest time. I went to my room to read the myth book, but I couldn't shake that soul-scraping emptiness John had opened up inside me. The very idea of losing my ma emptied me out.

I heard a door close and looked up to see Ma come into my room. "He's finally fallen asleep."

Lumbering around like a newborn colt, I spun to get up and hug Ma. She hugged me right back, letting out a laughing sigh. "Don't you worry, Nathaniel. I'm not going anywhere."

And for the first time, I hoped John Worth didn't have to go anywhere either.

17

Cattle and Chances

Come evening, I heard cows bellowing. Thinking they'd come through the fence again, I shouted for John, then made for the yard. The front door hung open, Ma standing on the stoop with her hands crossed over her chest. Knowing she wouldn't stand by to watch cattle trample our crops, my fear turned to confusion and I sidled up to Ma. Gavin Tussler, Mr. Clemson, and Pa herded a small group of cattle past our barn, then pushed them through the gate to our back pen. They milled around in there like a pack of hound dogs kept in a corn crib, all crowded together and noisy.

By then, I was close enough to holler, John right beside me. "Pa!"

"Howdy, Nate, John," Mr. Clemson called out as he

led his horse toward us. Mr. Tussler closed the gate. Pa turned our way.

"Evening, Mr. Clemson!" I yelled back. John nodded. "These cattle ours, Pa?"

Smiling and looking at me, Pa said, "That's right. Seth here said he'd pay for the crops in cattle." Mr. Clemson nodded to confirm it. "And we've got ourselves a bull coming as soon as we can build him a pen."

Cattle. A bull. I knew just what I was looking at with all those dirt stomping steer in our pen. But I let Pa tell me all about it as he put up the horse, then headed into the house. "We'll sell ten head off for beef this fall, then keep the five and the bull. Those five become ten come spring. We keep all we can that year, and before you know it, we have enough beef to tide us over when the harvest falls short."

"A herd!" Ma coughed as we came in.

Made me mad to have her anger raining in on the warmed-up feeling I had with Pa talking to me just like he used to when he had a farming plan in the works.

Pa winked at me. "Your Ma doesn't take to cattle."

"Cattle!" Ma turned, a spoon in hand. Pointing, she said, "You wouldn't go to Seth Clemson for the money he owed us. But you'd take his cattle and turn every farmer in the county against us. This makes us ranchers, Gabriel. Ranchers!"

Pa laughed. "You say that like we've become cattle thieves."

"Where are they going to graze?"

"With Clemson's cattle. We've got an agreement. Wrote it up and signed it with Mr. Carter to make it legal."

Pa hadn't gone to the bank for money. He'd gone to file his claim on the cattle.

"Well, you better hope Clemson's also willing to help you with the harvest. You won't find any farmers willing to pitch in to help a rancher."

"We're not ranchers, Mary Eve. We've got a few head of cattle. Not even enough to call a herd. Besides, it's not like we're the only folks taking such a deal."

"We're not?"

"There was practically a line at the bank. Widow Kerensky paid the Harpers in cattle. The Dales gave twenty head to the Planicks. There's cattle changing hands all over the county, Mary Eve. Won't nobody hold it against us."

Ma shook the spoon at me. "You stay clear of that bull, Nathaniel. That beast could tear you limb from limb."

John sniggered.

"You too!" Ma shouted, making him jump.

Pa laughed, then he got a good look at John. "Looks like you've been pretty tore up already."

John bowed his head.

I held my breath for a second, then said, "I hit him."

Pa stood over John. "Hit him? You nearly knocked his eye through the back of his head." He lifted John's chin to have a good look.

"I'm sorry."

Pa gave me a side look, then asked John, "What started this?"

"A misunderstanding."

"Uh-huh." He looked at me. "And you've worked this out?"

"Yes, sir," I answered. John nodded as Pa let go of his chin.

"Good."

"That's all you're going to say?" Ma asked. "Your son beats a boy bloody and you leave it at that?"

"I'm letting the boy fight his own battles. He's got to learn it some time."

Ma shook her head, then marched to the bedroom. Passing me, she said under her breath, "A man fights a battle with his mind, not his fists."

As she went into her room, Pa yelled, "A mind doesn't do you much good when you're staring down a fist, Mary Eve!"

"Wouldn't come to that if men would use their heads!"

"We'll leave her in the company of her ideas, boys." Pa patted my shoulder. "Let's go have a look at those cattle."

Pa kept staring at my leg as we headed to the barn. He gave a quick look at John, saying, "Sorry it had to be at your expense, John, but Nate . . ." Pa gave my back a good swat. "Darn proud of you for holding your own. And then some."

At the fence, we watched the cattle mill around, stirring up dust and knocking into the wood. "We'll have to build a bigger pen. Then we can give this one to the bull." Standing on the fence, he looked down at me. "You could probably help with that, Nate. Not a lot of traveling around with fence building."

"All right." The idea of it had me full to bursting. Gave me the strength to pull myself right up to next to him.

As John pulled up on the other side, Pa asked, "So what did set you boys to fighting?"

John looked to the barn. "I thought Nate was laughing at the way I pitched."

"Well, you do look like you're trying to shovel snow."

"I know," John mumbled.

"And what were you laughing at?" Pa asked me.

"A silly idea I had."

"And all this is worth punching each other?" Pa frowned.

"It got a mite uglier than that," I said.

"I called him a cripple."

Pa gripped the fence until the wood groaned. "You best choose your words more carefully, Mr. Worth, or I'll take my hand to you."

"Yes, sir."

Pa stepped down. "Clean the stalls when you're done gawking. We got work to do come dawn."

"Yes, sir."

My insides kind of split into pieces as Pa stepped off that fence. Part of me felt heart good that he defended me, but then the shame of my leg had sent him walking. Another part of me hated how twisted up and sad John looked knowing he treated a pitch like a shovel and he'd made Pa mad enough to leave.

Having my feelings pulled in every direction wasn't any better than just plain hating John Worth. Darn if he didn't find a way to make things worse just when I thought they had a chance of getting better.

18

What We Learn

Pa had John at work before sunup, so they'd already eaten and gotten to work before I even woke up. Getting ready, I checked every window to see if I could find them, to know if they were starting the pen without me.

As she set my plate down, Ma said, "Your father will be putting up the new fence tomorrow so you won't have to miss any school."

"I'm glad to be helping," I said, bursting my egg yolk with my biscuit.

Ma smiled. "I can tell. You've got a hearty appetite just thinking about it."

And the thought of it made school tolerable. Even when the upper grades had to make recitations of the Preamble to the Constitution. That thing doesn't hardly make sense on its own. Hearing kids stumble and choke their way through it a dozen times makes it into so much ear-cracking noise after a while.

My brain was so numb any old thing became interesting. Horace Danver got up to speak, and I saw a flash of skin as he sauntered down the aisle in his blue flannel shirt. He did more work with his arms than with his mouth. He gestured like a street hawker with the tear in his shirt flapping like a tongue. I found myself actually watching that old fabric with interest until my mind reached back to those Greek myths. All those silly speeches faded away behind Hydras, Minotaurs, and Medusas. I even imagined myself fighting them with my sword. When that Hydra showed up, so did John, torch at the ready like Iolaus, burning the necks as I cut off the heads so they couldn't grow back.

I couldn't wait to get back home and read more of them myths. Then Mr. Kennel showed up with his ruler. Slapping the hand resting on my good leg, he asked, "What's so interesting that you can't pay attention to these recitations, Mr. Peale?"

He startled me into talking before I could think. I held up the book. "This here book."

Everybody laughed until it made my head swim.

"I see. If it is so good, why don't you read to us?" Mr. Kennel crossed his arms in front of him like he was pleased to make a fool of me.

I took in a breath, then gave it a try. I read from the story of Persephone, the girl Hades dragged into the Underworld. I got another round of laughter when I tried to pronounce her name. I said, "Per-sep-*hon*-ey."

Mr. Kennel said, "Persephone."

I kept reading and the room fell quiet. I thought they'd fallen asleep. But when I put the book down they were actually listening.

"You've done a fine job with your reading, Mr. Peale. Well done," Mr. Kennel said, then that ruler-snapping fellow actually clapped—giving folks permission to do the same.

I had a whole room of folks clapping at me for reading. Had me so jumping happy, I nearly galloped to catch up to Anemone after school—slide, slide, slide. I could move pretty fast that way.

I slid up right beside her. "Can I keep the book for a while longer?"

She smiled and said I could, saying, "Thank you for

sharing that story with the class. Now they know, good things come from Greece."

"Parakalo." I tried my hand at a little Greek.

She laughed, but she didn't correct me, so I figured I'd gotten it pretty close to right.

I headed out toward the mercantile with her right alongside, grumpy old Alexander a few steps off so's no one knew he was following. She asked, "Which story did you like the best?"

"Well, I like that one about Dead and his son Icky flying up to the sun."

Anemone laughed like I'd just licked an icy pole. "Daedalus and Icarus."

"Huh?"

"Their names are Daedalus and Icarus."

"You don't say?" She had me turning a shade darker than a beet. I could feel the heat of it in my cheeks.

"I like that story too. But I also like the story of the golden ram that tried to save the children Phrixus and Helle. It was so sad that Helle fell to her death, but Phrixus reached safety."

"Ah, that's the ram that became the Golden Fleece that Jason and the Argonauts stole?"

"Yes."

"Some troublemakers, those Argonauts." I shuffled up to the boardwalk, beating Ma there. I turned around and realized I'd made it from school to the mercantile in a flash. I was getting pretty fast on my dead old leg.

"Yes." She laughed. "I'm glad you like the book."

"Thank you for lending it to me."

"Parakalo."

Ma appeared, saying, "Good afternoon, Anemone."

"Afternoon, ma'am." Anemone turned like she wanted to introduce her brother, but he'd already headed toward their house.

Ma handed her the pan, all fixed up. "Here you are."

"Oh," She turned it around, admiring it like it was a fine piece of glass. "Your husband does good work."

"Thank you." Ma gave that smile that always turned in my heart a little. The one that said, *I did this, not my husband, but thank you anyway.* "It's a dollar and a quarter for the mend, but I'll take that book Nate likes so much in trade. If your parents find that fair."

The book? Boy, howdy, would that be a trade worth dancing for.

Anemone nodded. "I will ask." Then she bowed her head a little, saying, "My *mana* would like to invite you to . . . to . . . to make bread with her."

"Make bread?"

"Yes, baking is a good time for women to talk, Mana says."

"Indeed. Tell your mother I can come any afternoon she cares to have me."

"Monday?" Anemone sounded uncertain, like she thought maybe Ma was just being polite.

"All right." Ma smiled.

"Great!" Anemone turned to run, calling back, "Good-bye!"

As we walked toward Belle, Ma said, "Mrs. Cordimas must be lonely."

"Being new to the country and all."

"That's right. And her daughter seems mighty nice." Now Ma was testing me.

"A lot better than her ornery brother." I liked Anemone, even liked the idea that her and my ma might be friends, but that didn't mean I had to let on.

"I see."

When we got home, Ma set to the tinker work she had spread across the table. John sat by the fireplace, picking slivers out of his hands. "We've been cutting wood from someone's barn all day."

"The Clarke barn," I said. Folks had been taking pieces of that old place since the Clarkes left the territory the spring before. Too many poor harvests had sent them back East.

"I hate the Clarkes." John sucked at his wounds.

"Want to read a few myths?" I asked, holding up the book that could soon be mine.

John stood up to agree, but Pa stepped in, saying, "No time for that, Nate. There's a town meeting I've got to get to, and John has to head down to the river and pick up a load of clay so we can start the fence posts."

"Clay?" John asked.

Pa got his "you're dumber than dirt" expression. He was about to speak, but I cut in, saying, "I can go with him, Pa. Show him how it's done."

Ma stood up. Catching the steel look in her eye, I said, "I'll stay on the wagon and tell him how it's done."

Seeing Ma's face soften, Pa said, "All right."

Sitting back down to her work, Ma said, "Be home by dark."

The thrill of heading out set off a tornado in my stomach. "Yes, ma'am." Swatting John, I said, "Hop to."

He followed me out, grumbling like I'd asked him to muck out the stalls after the cows ate too much clover.

I heard Pa say something to Ma, but I didn't have time to pay him any mind. He would take Vernon into town for the meeting, so I showed John how to hitch up Belle and Dimple. Well, I tried to show him, but my leg gave out on me, sending me into the hay bales alongside the barn. Scrambling to get up, I sat down real quick so Ma couldn't see me fumbling.

"You all right?" John asked.

My leg hopped like a frog struck by lightning. "Yeah."

"Does it hurt when it does that?" John pointed at the leg.

"Yes! Now get that harness on that cow before I put it on you."

He just stood there, holding the harness. "I used to wish my family could've survived the fire like Eddie

Dawson's ma, but then I saw her. Mrs. Dawson was half gone. Nothing but scarred-up stumps for hands, half her face all burned up, little hair to speak of. Her voice just gravel through her shrunk-up lips." He shivered. "Death's better than seeing your ma all chewed up like that. 'Grieving's for the selfish,' my granddad said. 'What right do we have to wish our family away from Heaven?'"

"Are you trying to say I should've died?" I'd thought it more than once myself, but having him say it made me mad enough to choke him with that harness.

"No." He took a step back. "You just got me thinking, that's all. Can't a man think around you?" He moved to harness Dimple.

"If he has thoughts worth listening to."

"Well then, I'll just keep my thoughts to myself."

"You do that."

And he did. Not one word did he say all the way to the river. Didn't say much else when I told him how to cut into the clay and haul it up, until he had a good number of the bricks in the wagon. "How many of these do we need?"

"Need two bricks for every fence post, at least, and

they come along every six feet. Pa probably wants a good one hundred twenty feet by one hundred twenty feet of walking room for those cows."

Scratching numbers into the dust on the seat, I started the math, but John jumped in right quick with, "We need one hundred sixty bricks? I'll be here until January!"

"How'd you do that?"

"Do what?"

"Come up with that figure so quick."

"Tossing nickels."

I couldn't see how throwing money made you good with sums, but John told me as he headed out to cut another brick. "See, you make bets on how far you can throw the nickel or what you can throw it on or in. Some of the fellows get into a game by tossing pennies, but not the game behind Santori's. It's a nickel or better to get in.

"Once you call your toss, you get odds. Like, I bet this nickel I can throw it in that old tin can over there. A guy says, 'I'll give you five to one.' That means he bets five nickels to your one. You win, you get the two bits. You lose, all he gets is your nickel. See the figuring?"

"Yeah." I was still adding fives when he said two bits, but I didn't need to let him know that.

John headed back to the clay but stopped halfway.

Thinking he'd been spooked by a snake in the grass, I whispered, "What do you see?"

Shaking his head, he said, "Things I wished I wasn't."

The way he closed his eyes tight told me he wasn't talking about anything on the prairie. I figured his mind was back in New York with his kin. Feeling a little like I'd stepped into a funeral without knowing the family, I stayed quiet.

Kicking clay, he said, "Pitching nickels. That's what I was doing when the fire started." His voice grew distant as if he'd traveled back in time, then it fell flat, drained of all emotion. "A man fell asleep with his pipe, they say. His bed caught fire. His wife turned from doing the dishes and saw her husband in flames. I hear he woke up screaming, but she ran from the building with her children to save their lives. There was no saving her husband."

Making that choice would crack a person's soul right down the middle.

He turned to the setting sun. "Pitching nickels is

what saved me. I'd lied to my ma, told her Mr. Santori'd give me a nickel to sweep up his shop. While I got all big headed over making a dollar seventy-five in nickels, my family got trapped inside that burning building."

I knew he had to tell the story through, but I'd rather have been buried alive in the clay at his feet than hear the rest.

"The fire escape fell apart. All those people running down the rusty old steps pulled it right off the building, trapping the other folks inside."

He looked at me, his face twisted with the pain of it.

In my mind, I could see those folks on the fire escape tumbling to the ground in a rush of screams and cracking metal. I held my breath against the horror of it all. The people on the top floors had no way out. The fire would eat them or they could jump to their deaths. I shuddered to think of John's sisters, who slept three to a bed, jumping from a window, their nightshirts billowing up around them as they fell. Grabbing my head to squeeze out even the thought of them falling to their deaths, I pushed words right out of my mouth. "Did they jump?"

John's face looked gray in the fading light. "They

turned up a bed and hid behind it, all huddled up like soldiers caught in the cold."

The wind that came up off the prairie could've blown me away like so much ash. I had nothing left to even imagine such a death.

We sat in silence until John jumped up, saying, "Awful price to pay for a ticket to heaven." He stabbed into the clay with the spade so hard I thought his shoulder would break. "That's what Granddad used to say."

"Where's your granddad now?" My thoughts raced to the idea John had a small piece of his family to turn to, but as soon as the words left my mouth, I knew I'd asked the wrong thing. If his grandfather was living, why'd he end up on an orphan train?

"He turned in his own ticket years ago, but he's seeing the truth of his words now."

"Uh-huh." I felt like such a fool. I had no better words to use, no way to let John know how sorry I was that he'd lost his family. How wrong it seemed that anyone should be robbed of life so brutally. The thought of it made it hard to take a breath. The whole of it was too awful, I had to force it out of my head so I could breathe again.

John seemed to be scrambling to follow the same

plan when he started to shout: "Five to one odds, that means I get a quarter from any fellow who took the bet. Ten to one odds, and I get fifty cents, but only suckers take that kind of bet. Most kids just bet two to one. You're only out a dime if you lose."

He wanted a way out of the memory, so I tried to help, asking, "Can you show me odds like that?"

"Huh?"

"Can you show me how to work up the numbers?"

John dropped a brick in the wagon, then walked up to my seat, all his grief flooding into a sense of longing, a need for escape. "I'll show you the numbers if you show me the words you know for reading. And," he pointed at me, "what you learn in history."

"You want to go to school?" What kind of escape was that?

"School? School's what got Willie Sharp a job. He got himself a diploma, went down and took a test, then had a job working numbers in a bank. From tossing nickels in an alley behind a pub to counting up money at a bank with one of them Oriental rugs big enough to fill your house. He even had his own room over at the Bilson. His own room."

"Yeah?"

"Yeah."

"You want yourself a job at a bank?" Couldn't imagine spending all my days inside. Just a few hours in that soddie made me see how folks could go crazed and run out into the freezing cold of the Nebraska prairie. I'd heard of folks who'd met their death that way.

John set back to work. "Yep. A bank or on the exchange or for one of them trading houses in New York. You can get a job writing slips to tell folks what cargo's coming in to what port. If you can read, write, do your sums, and show them a diploma, you got yourself a ticket to the good life."

"So you're going back to New York?"

"Soon as your pa lets me loose."

"You're not a slave."

He dropped a brick into the wagon. "Really, then what am I doing now?"

"If I wasn't lame, I'd be doing the same thing."

"And you think your pa's gonna give me land like he will you? No sir, I'm here for the work. Your pa told me so."

"He did?"

Deepening his voice to sound like Pa, he said, "Boy, you're here to do your share around the farm. For that you'll get meals and a bed. Don't expect more. Now or down the road." Going for another brick, he said, "Down the road's when he's passed on and giving over his land. You get the land."

He looked straight at me. I could see the hard edge in his eyes. The edge that said, "I work my hands until they're raw for my whole life, then you get the land I've worked. Where's the fairness in that?"

Even I could see there was no fairness in it. Only blood. I had my pa's blood in me. John didn't.

"Well, a bank job sounds good."

"You don't say. But I won't be getting a bank job if I can't keep up in my studies to get a diploma."

"I'll help."

"Good." He said it in a way that made me see that he figured I owed it to him. And even though he made me mad for thinking it, he was right.

19

Fence Cutting

I got down and climbed the bluff to keep my mind off how my darn leg had torn up my life and John's. Didn't see much but waving grass and a setting sun. My leg got to trembling, so I lay down, watching the sky turn as red as the clay John was cutting. Then I caught sight of somebody moving through the grass.

What's he up to? I thought, watching the fellow skulk through the grass like he might be stalking a pheasant or something. Wouldn't catch nothing but air with his bare hands. As he got closer, I could see he carried something, but what could he shoot in the dying light?

I felt like a hawk watching a prairie dog skittering through the grass. Then I saw the blades. The blades of shears. That fellow was a fence cutter!

"John!" I shouted, keeping it low so the fence cutter couldn't hear me.

He didn't answer.

Crawling on my elbows, I went to the edge of the bluff and shouted again.

"What?" John snapped. "I've only got half of these stupid bricks."

"Come up here. I see a fence cutter!"

"What?" John scrambled up the bank.

Hunkered down on the bluff, we could see the fellow heading for the Clemson fence line. I could see the blue of the fellow's shirt as clearly as I'd seen Mr. Tussler's scarf just days before. I'd seen Horace Danver reciting in that shirt just the other day. "That boy. It's Horace Danver. He's trying to start a war." He'd probably ripped his shirt when he'd cut fences the week before.

"How can you tell from here?" John asked. "It's practically dark."

"Free up Belle. We better get down there. Won't be but a handful of folks to round up cattle with that town meeting."

"That was probably the plan," John yelled, heading down the bluff to free Belle.

I slid down after him. Using the wagon, I was up on Belle in a flash. John stared at me like I'd jumped on a dragon. "What?"

"I've never ridden a horse."

"There's always a first time. Now get up here!"

John scrambled up, then wrapped himself around me like he thought I could keep him from falling off.

"Loosen up. If you want to hold something, hold my leg down so I don't spook the horse." He kept one arm around my waist, then put his hand on my thigh. I hee-yahed Belle into a run. John nearly pulled us both off, but we had a lot of ground to cover to catch up to Horace Danver before he cut the fence.

He could have heard us coming last Tuesday the way the prairie grass sang as we whipped through it. Seeing us, he ran for the horizon, but no man's legs are a match for a horse. So we rode up on him just before he reached the fence line. "Jump," I shouted to John, holding on with all the strength I had.

John jumped, kicking me in the back as he went over, but he tackled Horace like a calf at branding time. Only trouble was, he didn't keep him on the ground. An old hand at fighting, Horace came up punching. He had John flat out before I could get Belle turned around, because my jumping leg had her side stepping and confused.

"Horace Danver!" I shouted.

He turned, his right fist at the ready, his left hand on John's collar.

John swept Horace's legs out from under him. He spun over to get to his feet, but Horace got to his own just as fast. I headed right between them with Belle, both boys throwing themselves a few steps back to get out of the way.

"Grab the shears," I shouted, kicking Horace in the chest to send him to the ground. He crawled after the shears. Already on his feet, John got there first.

"What you want these for, Danver?" John sliced into the air with the shears. "A little fence cutting?"

"Won't do you much good to stop me." He charged off into the tall grass. And his words ran right through me. If Horace knew everyone was in town for a meeting, so did whoever had joined him on the night of the first fence cutting.

John started to run after him.

"No time! We've got to get into town, warn the others!" I headed Belle toward the fence.

John did a balancing act on the wire to get on Belle. He caught his leg on the fence as he got up. He screamed like it'd torn his leg off, but I didn't have time to check. We ran full out into town, knowing all the while that fence cutters were heading for fences near about as fast.

Short of riding Belle up the church steps, I couldn't get inside fast enough, so I pushed John off her back, yelling, "Get them home! Minding their fences!"

"Will do!" John shouted, rushing up the steps, screaming, "Fence cutters! Fence cutters!"

The building came alive with rushing men, shouting and asking questions, running for their horses or their wagons. The whole place cleared out faster than a building on fire. As Pa and Mr. Clemson came out, I yelled, "Caught Horace Danvers cutting fence on the Southwest corner."

"Good to know!" Mr. Clemson shouted at a run.

"Well done, boys!" Pa yelled from a few steps behind him.

John looked up at me in a panic.

"Well, come on. We got some more fence cutters to

hunt up!" I rode Belle up to the church railing.

"Yee-ha!" John climbed up, then leapt on to the horse. Belle whinnied in surprise, then took off with the touch of my heels—she felt left out of the fray and wanted to catch up. And the hunt was on.

20

The Hunt

Pa and Mr. Clemson would cover our property lines, so we headed south knowing the Widow Kerensky didn't have much help around her place. Felt like we really were Hercules and Iolaus, hunting down the evildoers. Taking the east fence line, I yelled at John to keep his eye out for any cutters. I watched the fence line ahead, praying we wouldn't run straight into a stampede. My leg started cramping, so I rode close to the mane to cut into the pain and hold my seat.

"There!" John shouted, pointing to the southeast corner. A boy crouched at the fence line, looking no bigger than the kids who sat next to me at school. I set to whooping to scare the kid off. Worked so well, he dropped the cutters and ran, his hat flying off as he fled. Staring at that little straw hat, I realized we'd spooked

Milton Harper, the kid who tore the legs off bugs.

"That was Milton Harper. He's like seven or eight."

"Boys are doing the cutting," John said. "Why?"

"You've got me there." The pain in my leg stabbed into my hip. Near about passed out.

John shook me, saying, "Nate. Nate. Stay with me. I don't know the way back."

"I got to get down." Leaning to my good side, I fell off rather than slid off. The fall sent me to screaming again.

John danced around like he was the one hurting. "What if that boy sends someone out here?"

Panting through the pain, I yelled, "Cut the fence and let the cattle trample them." I didn't mean it of course.

My screams brought the widow herself in her buggy with a shotgun. She had John in her site too.

Just beyond my own shouts, I could barely hear John praying up a storm as she pointed the gun at him. He had me wondering if he might pray to join his family or to stay alive awhile longer.

Getting out, she kept her gun on John, then sidestepped to me, the screaming banshee in her grass.

"Who's that down there? What's happened to you?"

I shouted, "It's my leg!"

"Nathaniel Peale. How'd you get all the way out here?" I thanked my stars for all the tinkering Ma did for the widow. She not only gave us a serving bowl and a kitchen chair, but it meant she trusted me. She never even suspected I could've been using those shears on the ground. Of course, my bad leg helped my case a load.

"Horse."

"All the riding's got him hurting," John said. "But we scared off a cutter."

"You did?" She lowered her gun.

I screamed.

"Heavens. Let's get this child in the buggy." She jumped into action, getting me to the wagon with John's help. Tying Belle to her wagon, she took us home. So much for the hunt. Some Hercules I turned out to be.

21

A Little Pride to Bring Us Together

"Riding around the countryside like a couple of bandits," Ma said, rubbing my leg to quiet the muscles. "Leaving the cow and the wagon out by the river to be driven off. You're lucky those boys didn't hurt you!"

Biting down on my pillow to bear the pain, I spit it out, then said, "Milty Harper is seven, Ma. What's he going to do, spit on us until we drown?"

John thought that was really funny, but Ma wasn't amused, so he covered his mouth.

"What are those boys doing cutting fences, anyhow?"

I said, "If you ask me, it's revenge for Calvin's death. Horace wants someone to pay for losing his brother. He doesn't care who."

"I *was* asking you." Ma rubbed my head. "And you're probably right. He roped in little Milton Harper and who knows who else. You did a good thing tonight, Nathaniel." Patting my chest, she said, "A good thing."

"You too." Ma smiled at John. He looked proud enough to be a new pa.

Putting the warning back into her voice, she said, "But if you two go running off like lawmen again, I'll lock you away until you can grow beards."

"Yes, ma'am," we shouted together.

Ma asked, "How's your leg?"

"Better." I said it only because I wanted her to stop rubbing the thing. I swear her hands turned as red hot as the metal she melted when she rubbed my leg.

"I'll make you dinner." She stepped out and John moved over to the bed.

"We're heroes." He looked like he expected to get a medal.

"Don't go strapping on your six-shooters just yet, Wyatt Earp. I've got to go to school with those boys come Monday."

"What makes you think they'll go to school?"

"They're kids."

"That Horace fellow's got to be sixteen if he's a day.

They'll clinch him. And if they can prove he cut those fences, he might be meeting the end of a rope."

"This is Nebraska, not New York City." Then I remembered. This was Nebraska. Home of Judge Lynch himself. "Ma!"

"What is it?" Ma rushed into the room like she expected to see my leg had come clean off or something.

"They won't lynch those boys, will they?"

"Not with their fathers around."

Feeling the relief clear down to my toes, I sank back into bed.

"Hanging or no hanging, they won't just send those boys back to school."

"Good. Then maybe I can get some work done."

John laughed.

But my mind had gone all mushy from the pain. I just kept right on sinking until I fell asleep.

Pa woke me with the shout, "Where are my boys?"

Startled, I didn't have much time to think on what he'd said, but he came right into my room and scooped me out of bed to carry me into the kitchen, Ma shouting all the while that I needed to rest. "This boy!" He raised me up, then seeing John, he stepped over to salute us both. "These boys stopped a range war. Talk about using your head, Mary Eve. These boys ran straight to town to warn us. Didn't stop there, though. Scared off a fence cutter on the Kerensky place."

"Then flopped around in her grass like a fish out of water," I said.

"No different than the marshal who goes after his man even after the dirty cur shoots him. He still gets the job done before he gives in to pain."

Made me feel heart good to be in Pa's arms, seeing his joy, feeling his heart beating against my arm. Ma rolled her eyes at us. But it even felt mighty nice to have John standing there with us, smiling away.

22

The Fences We Build

Turned out, Horace Danver had recruited himself a little schoolyard army to start a war. The men who rode out from the town meeting caught up with near to a dozen fence cutters. Those who weren't caught in the act were ratted on by the scared boys who'd been captured. By dawn, every one of them was facing the wrath of their fathers, some of them sent off to military school, some sent to work on the farms they'd nearly destroyed. And work was what I had in mind myself.

Pa made me up a special kind of crutch. I leaned on it when I worked, but it had a flip-down seat with its own two legs. When my leg got to throbbing, I just had myself a sit-down on that thing. I could move around and take a rest any time I needed. Once I rested up, I dove in again, John holding the fence in the middle, Pa and I hammering on both ends. Worked out mighty fine.

Folks stopped in all day to thank us for sounding the alarm. Pa watched them shake our hands and pat us on the back, soaking it all in with a smile on his face so big it near about ran off the edges.

Doc Kelly drove out to check my leg. The scar looked red enough to start a fire, and it felt about the same. "Nice work there, Gabe." He knocked on the crutch. "He needs to stay off this leg for at least a week."

"A week?" I dreaded the idea of being stuck in bed.

"I've got good shoulders," Pa said, holding out his arms.

I'd shown Pa I could hold my own, so now he was willing to carry me. Made me feel six parts proud and six parts angry that he didn't see that right off. Then again, I hadn't seen it myself, so how could I fault him?

Even Mr. Danver came by, hat literally in hand. "I may have my differences with the Gantrys, Mr. Peale, but I don't take to low-down tactics. If you're amenable, Horace will be here to help you with the harvest. For free."

"It was the Clemson fence he was about to cut, Mr. Danver."

"And your crops that would've been ruined."

"Sounds fair, then." Pa held out his hand.

Mr. Danver shook it. "I'm a fool for saying it, but God's already heard it echoing in my head. I'm so glad he didn't cut on Gantry land. I can't lose another son."

Pa nodded, looking from me to John. "I know the feeling."

Mr. Danver squeezed Pa's hand all the tighter. "I see that you do."

Horace's dad walked off as stoop shouldered and sad as Pa looked when he left for the barn after I'd been hurt. A father feels the weight of his son's pain. No matter what its source.

"I'm doing good, Pa."

"Of course you are." Pa turned to the fence. "Let's get cracking."

And we set to work, no one really talking, no one really saying John Worth was now a son, one of the family for doing his part in saving our farm and keeping me safe, but I saw it in the look Pa gave John when Mr. Danver talked of losing a son.

There was no telling what Pa would do when it came time for John and me to inherit or what John might do when he grew old enough to go back to New York City, but for now we were a family.

And I had a brother. A brother to swap stories with, who'd learn about history from me and teach me how to do my sums. Come winter, when the work around the farm grows as thin as bare trees, Pa might even let him go to school with me.

As I listened to the wind bending over the prairie grass, I realized I'd never have my leg as good as new. Ma would never hold her Missy again. John couldn't see his family until the Lord called him home, but we'd make do with what we had. And what we had was pretty darn good.

About the Author

A. LaFaye (the "A" is for Alexandria) is the author of *The Year of the Sawdust Man, Nissa's Place, The Strength of Saints, Edith Shay, Strawberry Hill,* and *Dad, in Spirit.* She teaches at California State University at San Bernardino during the school year and at Hollins University in Roanoke, Virginia, in the summer.